W9-AVM-019

09/12

Eva of the Farm

Eva of the Farm

Dia Calhoun

Atheneum Books for Young Readers

New York   London   Toronto   Sydney   New Delhi

ATHENEUM BOOKS FOR YOUNG READERS
An imprint of Simon & Schuster Children's Publishing Division
1230 Avenue of the Americas, New York, New York 10020

For information about special discounts for bulk purchases, please contact Simon & Schuster
Special Sales at 1-866-506-1949 or business@simonandschuster.com.
The Simon & Schuster Speakers Bureau can bring authors to your live event. For more
information or to book an event, contact the Simon & Schuster Speakers Bureau at
1-866-248-3049 or visit our website at www.simonspeakers.com.
Book design by Sonia Chaghatzbanian
The text for this book is set in Goudy Old Style.
Manufactured in the United States of America
0612 FFG
First Edition
2 4 6 8 10 9 7 5 3 1
Library of Congress Cataloging-in-Publication Data
Calhoun, Dia.
Eva of the farm / Dia Calhoun. — 1st ed.
p. cm.
Summary: Twelve-year-old Eva writes beautiful poems on the farm in Washington State that
her family has owned for generations, but when money runs out and then her baby brother
gets sick, the family faces foreclosure and the way of life she loves is threatened.
ISBN 978-1-4424-1700-7
ISBN 978-1-4424-1702-1 (eBook)
[1. Novels in verse. 2. Loss (Psychology)—Fiction. 3. Farm life—Washington (State)—Fiction.
4. Poetry—Fiction. 5. Imagination—Fiction. 6. Family life—Washington (State)—Fiction.
7. Washington (State)—Fiction.] I. Title.
PZ7.5.C35Ev 2012
[Fic]—dc22
2010051917

For Lorie Ann Grover,
for telling me I am a poet;
and for Justina Chen,
for telling me I can fly.

Acknowledgments

First, I would like to thank Karen Hesse, for believing in this book and offering inspiring encouragement. I would also like to thank my editor, Kiley Frank, for her brilliance and warmth. Thanks to my agent, Steven Chudney, for his steadfast faith. Thanks to Kathryn O. Galbraith, Lorie Ann Grover, Joan Holub, and Joan Soderland Hommel for critiquing the manuscript. Thanks to Shaula Zink, my sister-in-law, for sharing her expertise with stone bead jewelry. Thanks to Jim and Eva Calhoun, my parents, for their encouragement. Thanks to Arthur Zink, my father-in-law, for sharing the Farm. And finally and most of all, thanks to Shawn R. Zink, my husband, for everything in the world.

Eva of the Farm

On top of the hill,
I lean against the deer fence
and write a poem in the sky.
My fingertip traces each word
on the sunlit blue—
the sky will hold the words for me
until I get the chance
to write them down.
After the last line,
I sign my name—
Eva of the Farm.

My real name is Evangeline
after the heroine
in an old poem—
Evangeline: A Tale of Acadie.
Even though I'm only twelve,
I dream of being a heroine
of shining deeds—
like Saint Joan of Arc
or Meg from *A Wrinkle in Time,*
but everyone just calls me Eva.

Dodging the sagebrush on the hill,
I walk on
beside the wire deer fence
that protects our farm.
My job is to check for holes
the deer may have dug
beneath the wire.
It takes an hour and a half
to walk all the way around the deer fence—
our land covers nearly a hundred acres.

Our farm is named Acadia Orchard
after the land in the old poem.
You'd think we grow ambrosia,
or something magical for gods and heroes,
but we only grow plain old apples and pears—
Galas and Anjous—
here in the Methow Valley
in Eastern Washington.

I like those words—
something magical for gods and heroes—
and stop to write them in the sky
so I won't forget.
I want to be a poet
with a shining imagination,

but whoever heard of a heroine-poet?
There's nothing heroic
about scribbling stuff
that nobody wants to read—
except maybe my mom,
who is crazy mad about poetry
and Greek mythology.

I don't show anybody
but Mom
my poems—
not my teachers,
not my friends,
definitely not my dad,
who thinks poetry is useless
because it can't save the world
from all its problems.

Before Grandma Helen died,
I shared all my poems with her—
sometimes she'd even help me
find the perfect word.
She wanted me to enter my poem
"Waking up at the Farm in Summer"
in a national poetry contest for kids,
but I couldn't bear the thought

of some stranger judging my poem
and stamping on it
with his big black boot.

Waking Up at the Farm in Summer

I wake
under a skylight
that shouts blue against my glad eyes.
Another sunny summer day!

I scurry
down the ladder from my bedroom loft
to the smell of Dad's blueberry pancakes
sizzling in the frying pan.

I grin
at our black Lab, Sirius,
with a Frisbee in his mouth—
waiting for the first toss of the morning.

I run
outside with the gray squirrels,
the deer, rabbits, and whip-poor-wills—
high-fiving the newborn world.

As I walk down the hill,
checking the last section
of the deer fence,
dust dances around my feet.
It is hot and dry up here.
I can see my house below,
rising like a wooden ship
in a sea of green lawn.
I can see the orchard,
ruffled with leaves.
I can see the white slash
of the hammock.
I can also see that the west gate
leading to the wild canyon
stands wide open.

In my head I hear Mom shout,
"Close the gate!"
That's the Golden Rule of the Farm:
Close the gates to keep
the deer out of the orchard.

Five gates stand guard
in the deer fence.
The east gate—

where we drive in from the highway.
The west gate—
where we hike up to the wild canyon.
The south gate—
where I go to play with Mr. Reed's dog.
The north gate—
where we pick wild asparagus in the Andersons' orchard.
And the fairy gate—
only three feet high, it leads to the old cherry tree
on the farm where my best friend Chloe used to live.

I think all these gates are chimeras—
that's a word from the Greeks
that I learned in a book today
while reading in the hammock.
It means figments of your imagination.
Because if something really wants
to get into the orchard,
it will find a way through the gates,
through the deer fence.
I'm happy there is such
determination
in the world.

Sometimes, I want to fling all the gates wide open
to see what might come in.

Unicorns? Dragons? Centaurs?
Maybe then we'd get a little excitement around here.
Even Dad, who, in my humble opinion,
doesn't have much imagination at all,
might like to see a unicorn eating apples
by the hammock.

After closing the west gate,
I slide into the hammock,
swing and swing,
and remember the poem
I wrote yesterday.

Hammock Queen
In the hammock
I am a queen
in a swinging throne of string
borne by two tall knights—
the maple trees.

I toss dried corn
to my grateful subjects—
gray squirrels who peer
and chatter at me,
paying homage.

On my right stands
the boundary of my kingdom—
the tall deer fence.
Beyond it the wild world
of the canyon threatens—
beckons—
riddled with dragons,
promises of shining treasure,
and perilous quests.

But here,
on my side of the fence, is the Farm—
with rows of apple trees
lined up like soldiers.

Here, in a throne of string,
beside the wild world,
I sway,
stricken to the heart with earth and sky,
knowing,
I belong to this, my apple kingdom.

A wet nose nudges my arm
just as my eyes flutter closed
in the hammock.
"Hello, Sirius," I say to our black Lab.

I rub his ears,
silky as the yarn Grandma Helen spun
on her spinning wheel.
"You are a good and noble dog, Sirius," I say.
His tail thumps on the grass.

I jump out of the hammock.
Mom and Dad will be waiting
for my report on the deer fence.
With Sirius following,
I cross the yard,
passing the vegetable garden,
passing the blue spruce trees,
their branches fluttering with quail.

I walk toward the big new shed
that we built last spring
for the farm equipment, shop,
and office upstairs.
Sirius trots behind me
through the door to the shop
where Dad kneels beside our new tractor,
changing the oil.

I remember picking out the shiny orange tractor
with Mom last spring,

remember being astonished by the prices
on the dangling tags.
"Look at all those zeros," I'd said. "Do we
really have that much money?"
"No," Mom had said. "But the bank does.
We're taking out a loan to buy the tractor
and build the new shed."

Dad, still kneeling beside the tractor,
looks at the oil dripping into the pan.
"At least this new tractor
doesn't burn oil like the old one.
That's one more thing we've done
to help save the environment."
He pushes up his round, gold-rimmed glasses,
which are always sliding down his nose.

Mom, who is fixing a sprinkler valve,
glances up at me and asks,
"How is the deer fence?"
"No holes," I say. "The deer fence is strong."
"Good," Dad says.
Mom and Dad work the Farm together,
but they're always looking for ways
to make more money—

especially now that the economy
is bad,
and our neighbors—the Quetzals—
lost their farm.
Chloe Quetzal, my best friend,
had to move far away
over the lonely mountains
to Seattle.
I can't imagine losing our farm,
or moving to the city.

To make extra money,
Dad guides white-water rafters
on the Methow River in the summer
and teaches skiing during the winter.
Mom writes fishing, hunting,
and gardening articles
for magazines.
She hunts in fall and winter.
So we eat venison and
duck,
duck,
duck,
and more duck,
and quail and grouse, too.

My brother, Achilles—
named, what a surprise,
after the Greek hero Achilles—
chews on a plastic ring
in his playpen in the shop.
When I pick him up,
he raises his chubby arms,
grabs my nose,
and grins his lopsided grin.
A nine-month-old baby,
he mostly howls and poops.
He's cute when he is sleeping,
which doesn't happen often enough,
in my humble opinion—
Grandma Helen used to say
"in my humble opinion"
all the time.

I leave the shed,
go into the house,
and climb the ladder to my loft bedroom—
a fancy way of saying attic.
I call it the Crow's Nest.

With the skylight flung open,
I look at the sky—

it still holds the poem
I wrote up on the hill
by the deer fence.
To retrieve the words,
I stand still,
so still,
watching,
waiting,
until—
I am blueness,
I am cloud,
I am wind—
I am the sky.

Then the words of my poem
come flying back to me.
They are warm,
as though sprinkled
with all the spices of the sky.
When the poem is all inside my head again,
I write it down
in my best calligraphy.

I write all my poems
in calligraphy in black ink
on white Canson calligraphy paper.

Grandma Helen taught me
to shape the graceful letters
and hold the pen lightly
at a constant angle
in spite of my being left-handed.
I love the whisper of the pen
on the paper.
It makes me remember Grandma Helen.

The Haunted Outhouse

Grandma Helen built
an outhouse with a view
of the sagebrush hills.
"Sitting pretty," she called it.
"Why not?"
She slapped white paint
on the boards,
carved a smiling moon
on the door,
and planted violets
on every side.

Last year, Grandma Helen died.

Now the outhouse door creaks

in the lonely wind.
The metal roof rusts
in the weeds
on the ground.

But sometimes,
in the moonlight,
through glimmering spiderwebs,
I think I glimpse
Grandma's ghost—
sitting pretty.

Early the next morning,
I walk up the canyon with Dad.
The canyon winds like a green snake
between the dry sagebrush hills
behind the Farm.
Up and up and up we go—
looking toward Heaven's Gate Mountain.

The canyon is beautiful.
Aspens—black-and-white Dalmatian trees—
and ponderosa pines
sway in groves
with the on-again-off-again creek
chanting through

like a prayer.
Quail skitter in the brush
and deer graze.

The canyon is dangerous, too.
Cougars, bobcats, and bears
prowl here sometimes,
so I am scared to go up alone,
scared to go through that gate
in the deer fence.
So I go with Dad,
who loves wild places
and wants to save them all.

As we walk along the creek,
I think about dryads and naiads—
those Greek spirits of wood and stream,
like Pan—
and wonder if the Farm and canyon
have spirits too.
I wish I could ask Chloe
what she thinks.

Before Chloe moved away,
we explored the canyon together.

She filled her sketchbook
with pencil drawings
of flowers, leaves, birds, and bugs.
Once she even drew a dead rattlesnake.
Me—I can't draw to save my life.
Chloe knows all the common names
of every plant and insect,
and all their Latin names, too.

I haven't seen Chloe
for five long months,
but we'll be together again in
six weeks,
two days,
and ten hours—
for summer camp in Mazama in August.
We've gone to Camp Laughing Waters
every year since we were five.

When Dad and I reach
the first meadow in the canyon,
we find a half-eaten deer
sprawled across the trail.
Her throat is a bloody gash
torn by hungry teeth.

A sour stink already rises
from her guts
savaged across the dirt.

"Wow!" Dad exclaims, pointing.
"Look at the baby deer in the womb."
On the ground
lies a blob
as white and transparent as tapioca pudding.
Inside, pokes
the delicate hoof
and head
of the baby fawn—
dead.
Sickened, I turn away,
glad Dad didn't bring Achilles
as he sometimes does,
in the baby backpack.

"Coyotes killed this deer," Dad says,
"or maybe a cougar.
We've scared them away
from their breakfast."
I spin around
searching for the gleam of wild gold eyes
in the brush.

"I know this is brutal, Eva," Dad says,
scanning the ground for prints,
"but that cougar or coyote has its own babies
to feed.
It's just the wheel of life, turning."
I scan the bowl of hills and say,
"Let's go home."

On the crest of the south hill
a black snag—
the tall, spiky stump of a dead tree—
points at the sky.
Lightning must have struck it
during a storm long ago.
Suddenly I see that storm
in my imagination:
A hundred lightning bolts
fracture the sky
into a skeleton of light.
One bolt strikes the tree—
it stands—
trembling,
crackling,
absorbing
unimaginable power.

I blink,

and now I see that the black snag

looks like someone

wearing a black robe with a hood.

My skin creeps and crawls—

the stink of the dead deer

rising around me—

because I know,

just know,

that black snag has a powerful evil spirit.

One branch with a knob on the end

thrusts out like an arm

holding a black ball.

And it points straight at me.

The Demon Snag

Halfway up the canyon

the blackened snag on the hill

looms like a demon,

conjuring and cackling

evil dreams of the wild—

cougar teeth and bear claws and being eaten alive—

until fear cripples my heart.

I sharpen Dad's ax—
but a demon felled would be a demon still.
I call for a wizard,
but they are too busy fighting dragons.

If I were Joan of Arc,
I could defeat the Demon Snag myself
with a shining sword.
But I am only Eva of the Farm,
armed with a shining imagination
that makes me run home fast.

I send Chloe an e-mail
about the dead deer and her baby.
For two long days I wait for an answer
from Seattle.
Finally Chloe replies,
"Don't send any more disgusting messages like that!"
I slump,
drop the half-eaten apple in my hand,
and stare at the computer screen
in the Crow's Nest.
The Chloe I know
would have dissected that dead deer.
The Chloe I know
would have whipped out her sketchbook

and drawn a hundred pictures of that dead deer.
The Chloe I know
is an explorer and mastermind of daring deeds.

Now she only sends one-sentence e-mails.

The screensaver flashes—
a picture of Chloe and me
standing by a canoe
at Camp Laughing Waters.
Chloe's long, curly blond hair—
princess hair—
blows in the wind,
mixing with my lank
red-brown hair.
Wreaths of wildflowers
crown our heads.
The picture looks like a scene
from a fairy tale.

I put one hand to my side.
Tucked beneath my ribs
is the jagged hole
from losing Grandma Helen—
frayed and sore around the edges.
Now Chloe stands on the edge

of that hole—
about to fall in,
about to rip it wider,
about to vanish forever too.

"Don't go away, Chloe," I whisper.
"Don't go away like Grandma Helen did."
But Chloe doesn't look at me,
doesn't hear me,
she only keeps smiling on the screensaver
with her hair blowing in the wind.

I sigh and turn away from the computer.

Heat grips the walls of the Crow's Nest.
I'm so hot you could fry an egg
on my forehead,
as Grandma Helen used to say.
The Crow's Nest is the hottest room in the house
in summer
and the coldest one
in winter.
I swing the skylight open
on the slanted wall
over my bed
and hope for a breeze

to come skipping in,
and one does—
a breeze so fierce
my sun hat
sails off the doorknob.

Outside, storm clouds bully Heaven's Gate Mountain
heading for the Farm.
I love the Crow's Nest when the wind
shrieks around the eaves.
It makes me think of Meg
from A *Wrinkle in Time*
shivering in her attic,
waiting for Mrs. Whatsit,
Mrs. Who, and Mrs. Which.

I climb down the ladder to find Achilles
to watch the storm with me.
He always laughs at thunder and lightning,
as a proper Greek hero should.
Mom sits huddled at the kitchen table
staring down at Grandma Helen's gold watch
in her hands.
Twelve emeralds—
twelve for the months of the year,
green for the Farm, Grandma Helen used to say—

sparkle around the watch face.
"Mom?" I ask.
She doesn't look up.
"Mom, what's wrong?"
Mom answers in a choked voice,
"Grandma Helen's watch stopped."

"Did you wind it?" I ask.
"Of course," she says. "It stopped.
Just . . .
stopped."
Her face locks up as tight
as a turtle in its shell—
she's trying not to cry.

My great-grandmother Nita
gave Grandma Helen that watch.
Just before she died,
Grandma Helen gave it to Mom.
Someday, Mom will pass it on to me.
She lets me wear the watch
on my birthday.
"Can't we get it fixed?" I ask.
Mom doesn't answer,
but tears fall down her face.

I run outside to find Dad.

He's not in the shop in the shed.

So I climb the stairs to the office

where Dad's computer hums.

A "Stop Global Warming" slide show

Dad made plays on the screen.

One slide says "No Farms No Food."

The next slide shows the Farm in spring,

the next, the Farm in summer—

and on through the rest of the seasons.

On the last slide, a polar bear

stands beside a melting glacier.

Where is Dad?

He could be anywhere.

Grandma Helen used to say

that when Dad got up in the morning

he hit the ground running.

He seems even busier since she died.

As the slide show repeats,

I guess where Dad is.

And I do find him,

outside in the tree nursery—

a garden where he plants

baby evergreen trees in brave rows.

When they grow big enough,
he transplants them around the Farm.

The branches on the baby trees dance
in the rebellious wind.
Dad plunks one little ponderosa pine
into the wheelbarrow.
"Where are you going to plant that one?" I ask.
"By the canyon gate," he says.
Then he adds, as I know he will,
"Plant a forest, save a polar bear.
Want to help?"
I shake my head. "A big storm's coming."

Dad looks up toward the black clouds
quilting Heaven's Gate Mountain.
"I hadn't noticed," he says.
"Mom's crying," I tell him,
"because Grandma Helen's watch stopped."
Dad frowns.
I add, "I think she's missing Grandma Helen again."
"She's always missing Grandma Helen," Dad says.
"It's been a year. I don't . . ."
His face sags. "I just don't know what to do anymore."
And he trundles the wheelbarrow away,
not toward the house,

but toward the canyon gate—
into the storm.

Summer Storm

Above Heaven's Gate Mountain
the wind curls
over the hot blue sun.

Across the hills
the pine trees roar—
sparkling, black-veined emeralds.

Deep in his den
the coyote shivers,
knowing there will soon be thunder.

Up the canyon
the aspens shimmy in the rain
pelting their white bark.

Along the deer fence
the beans snap,
and the corn careens across the garden.

In the sky
clouds ponderous as melons
begin their slow black calling.

From my skylight
I see the flash of a meadowlark
singing the bright memory of sunlight.

Achilles claps his hands
and croons when the storm
flings jagged pearls of hail
against the skylight.
When the hail finally stops,
rain parades
against the glass
on
and on
and on
while the robins
hop over the wet grass
and stuff their beaks
with worms.

So I build a block castle
for Achilles.
I plop his toy horse inside the castle walls
and tell him the Greek story
of the Trojan horse.
Achilles listens,
his eyes as big as robin's eggs,

as though he really understands.
At just the right moment in the story—
when the Greeks are sneaking out of the horse
to destroy the city of Troy—
Achilles reaches out with both hands
and knocks down the castle
I have so carefully built.
He shrieks and gurgles with glee.
"You're a true Greek hero, Achilles,"
I say, laughing.

When at last the rain stops,
the desert heat prowls
across the land again.
I'm glad we have a good well.
I'm glad the Methow River runs nearby.
Most of all,
I'm glad for the irrigation sprinklers.

Sprinklers

In this desert land
arcs of water—
silver rainbows—
pulse from a thousand sprinklers
day and night,

sweeping circles
around the apple and pear trees.

In this desert land
the apple and pear trees
are always thirsty,
always hot,
their wet green leaves
taunting the dry hills—
"nyah, nyah, na-nyah-nyah!"

In this desert land
if I am thirsty,
if I am hot,
I dance and drink
and grow dizzy
running through
the sprinklers.

In this desert land,
the water comes
from the Methow River—
so I think there should be fish
shooting out of the sprinklers
and into Dad's frying pan
for dinner.

A week later,
I walk out to the shed,
looking for Mom and Dad,
to tell them about
a pear tree with dead
leaves on one of its branches.

No one's in the shop.
Tools hang in orderly rows
from hooks on the walls—
saws, axes, hammers, wrenches,
coils of rope,
and a dozen pruning shears.

In one corner,
a blue sheet shrouds
what I know is Grandma Helen's spinning wheel.
It broke a month before
she got sick.
Mom hauled it into the shop,
planning to fix it.
But she hasn't touched the spinning wheel,
even though I've told her a hundred times
that I'd love to learn to spin,
like the three Fates in Greek mythology.

Dust rises
when I lift the blue sheet.
The spinning wheel is beautiful.
It should be turning,
should be spinning,
shouldn't have cobwebs
tangled in the spokes.
I used to write my best poems
to the sound of the wheel humming
while Grandma Helen spun.

Footsteps crunch in the gravel
outside the shop door.
The door creaks open
and Dad strides in,
his face grim.
"What's wrong?" I ask.
"Fire blight," he says.
My breath shoots into my lungs
as I remember the pear tree with dead leaves.
"How bad?" I ask.
"Terrible," he says.

He explains that
last week's hailstorm

gouged the bark on the pear trees.
More days of heat and rain
brought fire blight,
a horrible disease,
I know,
which might destroy
our entire pear orchard.

"I saw a pear tree
with a dead branch,"
I say.
"Where?" he asks.
"Down by the fairy gate."
Dad becomes a whirlwind,
pulling saws and axes
off their hooks on the wall.
"Then it's spread even farther
than I thought," he says.
"Looks like were in for a siege."

The Siege
Mom's saw, screeching.
Dad's ax, hewing.
My heart, aching.
Hour after hour,

day after day,
I pile dead branches
into the wheelbarrow
and trundle them
to the bonfire.

Only butchery
and burning
will keep the disease
from spreading
and stop
the fire blight—
maybe.

Our orchard
curls up in smoke
that stings tears
into my eyes
as I say good-bye
to my lost friends
the trees.

One night at dinner Dad says,
"The pear crop is mostly gone,
but we still have the apples."
His eyes are bloodshot from smoke.

"The Galas weren't touched by the blight."
But I know
we have only ten acres of apples.
I know
Mom and Dad borrowed all that money
for a loan from the bank
to buy the new tractor
and build the new shed.

I don't know
how we will pay the bank back.
I don't know
what we will do.
I don't ask,
but think of the Demon Snag
up the canyon
and wonder
if its evil power
caused the fire blight.

"The Gala crop is good," Dad says into the silence.

I stare down at the scrambled eggs
speckling my blue plate
for the fourth time this week.
"I'm tired of eggs," I say.

"Would you rather have duck?" Dad asks.
I shut right up.

"Have you finished your new poem
about the fire blight?" Mom asks me.
Dad frowns. "You should ask
if she's finished her summer math homework."
I hunch my shoulders,
sensing one of Dad's lectures,
and, sure enough, it comes.

"You're such a bright girl, Eva," he begins,
pushing up his gold-rimmed glasses.
"Your generation is facing so many problems—
like global warming
and species extinction.
You can't feed a poem
to a starving polar bear.
You can't use a poem
to stop tiger poaching.
The answers lie in math and science
and economics—
not poetry."

I've heard all this before,
but still something shrivels inside me

like a slug
when you pour salt on it.

Mom says, "Words can move hearts, Kurt.
A poem about the plight of the polar bears
might inspire people to help them.
We make the most difference
when we use the gifts we have.
And Eva is a gifted poet."

Dad's face softens.
"Of course she is," he says. "I just want you
to be a well-rounded person, Eva,
so you can take on the world
when you grow up—
and make a decent living.
I'm betting your average mathematician
earns more
than even a gifted poet."
I swallow a big bite of eggs
and say to defend myself,
"I *have* finished my summer math homework."

Mom changes the subject.
"Summer is half over.
"Tomorrow we'll go to the thrift shop in Twisp

to buy you new school clothes."

"And camp clothes, too," I say.
"I need new shorts."
Mom and Dad glance at each other,
Mom starts to speak,
but just then Achilles flings
his plate of eggs onto the floor.

I finger the hole in my shorts.
The clothes from the thrift shop won't be new,
but other people's hand-me-downs.
I like the thrift shop, though,
because anything is possible there.

Anything Is Possible

For three dollars
anything is possible at the thrift shop
at the Senior Center in Twisp.

For three dollars
you can stuff whatever you want in a bag.
The thrift shop has everything
you can imagine
and some things you cannot.

Clothes, dishes, toys, puzzles—
Mom can stuff a bag tighter
than our Thanksgiving turkey.
It's embarrassing.

For three dollars
I can stuff a new me
into the bag.
I can become a heroine
in a flowing red skirt
with only a little tear
that trails behind me on the floor—
and a ruffled white shirt
like Evangeline might wear.
I add silver boots and a silver helmet
with only a small dent,
like Joan of Arc might wear.
And I am ready for anything.

Three dollars
is too much for me to waste,
Mom says.
She dumps everything out of my bag
except the silver boots,
which I can wear in the snow.

She crams the bag with boring
T-shirts, jeans, and sweaters.

If Joan of Arc's mother
and Evangeline's mother
and Meg's mother
were anything like mine,
they would never
have had any adventures at all.

Tonight there will be a meteor shower
called the Perseids.
It happens every August
in the constellation of Perseus.
Everyone—
Dad, Mom, Achilles, Sirius, and me—
lies outside on the grass,
listening to the cricket symphony
and waiting for the shooting star show
to begin,
as we have every year
for as long as I can remember.
This year I'm especially excited,
because this is Achilles's first time
to watch the Perseids.

I want him to see
his first falling star—
his blue eyes opening wide in delight.
I want him to stretch
his hands toward the stars.

For a few hours I can forget
about the fire blight's rampage,
about Chloe's silence,
about Mom's grief,
about Dad's indifference,
about Demon Snags.
Forget.

As darkness falls,
I think about my last e-mail to Chloe.
I told her about the fire blight,
but she hasn't answered.
Not one sentence.
"I wish Chloe were here to watch
the show with us," I say to Mom and Dad.
"But at least I'll get to see her soon
at Camp Laughing Waters.
I can't wait!"

Mom and Dad exchange glances.

"Eva," Dad begins, but Mom interrupts.

"This isn't the best time to tell her, Kurt."

But Dad shakes his head. "There's no good time."

I sit straight up. "Tell me what?"

Mom's face is serious. "I'm afraid

there will be no summer camp this year."

My hands clutch the grass

as though I might fall off the world

if I don't hold on tight.

"What do you mean?" I ask. "Why?

Did the camp close?"

Dad sighs. "No. We just can't afford

to send you this year, Eva.

You know how bad things are—

with the fire blight ruining the pear crop.

Money is tight."

"Very tight," Mom adds.

"But"—my voice squeaks—

"I was going to see Chloe again."

Mom says, "Mrs. Quetzal called me yesterday.

Chloe isn't going to camp this year either.

She doesn't want to go."
My fingers claw even deeper
into the grass
as I say in a faint voice, "She doesn't . . .
want to go? Why not?"
"Sometimes," Mom explains gently,
"when people move away and begin new lives,
they also make new friends
and find new interests.
I think Chloe's done that.
I am so sorry, Eva."

"There!" Dad shouts. "I see a falling star!"

But I do not look up.
I fall back on the grass
and squeeze my eyes shut—
squeeze my fists shut—
squeeze my worry shut
tightest of all.

Falling Star
Falling
I shoot—

falling
I shine—
falling
I vanish
forever.

Cherries are my idea of heaven,
but we don't have a cherry tree.
We used to pick buckets from the tree
in Chloe's orchard
on the other side of the fairy gate.
Our new neighbors
haven't offered us any cherries,
and we don't have money to buy them—
cherries are expensive,
even at the farmer's market in Twisp.

Sometimes I think if I could taste
one cherry—just one—
the worry inside me
would go away,
and everything would be all right again,
and I could go to Camp Laughing Waters
with Chloe.
Cherries are that magical.

The Old Cherry Tree

A ladder sighs
against the old cherry tree
across the deer fence
in the neighbor's yard.
Cherries dangle
like ruby earrings
from the branches.

In spite of Mom's warnings,
I want to steal those cherries
and stuff them in my mouth.

The cherries taunt
beyond my outstretched fingers
while starlings jeer and dart,
pecking greedy holes in the fruit.

I long for thieving wings—
to steal such sweetness for myself.

On Friday morning
Mom and I drive to the post office
in Methow—
a town so small
a rabbit could pass it by

in one hop.
Mom leaves our old Ford truck running
while I go in and grab the mail
from our post office box.
I flip though the stack and find
  —a flyer for a free pizza,
    if you buy three large ones
    at the regular price
  —a letter from Dad's cousin in Seattle
  —a copy of the *Good Fruit Grower* magazine
  —a letter from the Methow Valley Community Bank
    with big red letters printed on the envelope:
    URGENT: FORECLOSURE NOTICE.

The envelope is as white as snow,
and a chill spreads from it
up through my fingers.
I've heard the word
"foreclosure," somewhere before.
Although I scrunch up my brain,
and think and think,
I can't remember where.

I put the letter from the bank
on top of the pile of mail
so Mom will see it right away.

I will ask her
what foreclosure means.

But when I climb back into the truck
and Mom sees the letter,
her face turns pale.
She snatches the letter,
stuffs it into her purse,
and then hunches over the steering wheel,
her pink lips pressed tight.

My breath speeds up,
coming short and fast.
My tongue sticks
to the roof of my mouth
as though I've eaten
a whole jar of peanut butter.
I'm too afraid to ask Mom
what foreclosure means.

Something is wrong—
terribly wrong.

When we get home,
I climb straight up to the Crow's Nest,
sit down at my computer,

and Google "foreclosure definition."
This is what comes up:
"Foreclosure is a legal proceeding
where the bank takes possession
of a mortgaged property
when the borrower is behind
on loan payments."

A hot nail seems to scrape
down my spine as I slump in my chair.
What I have been afraid of
since the fire blight struck
is true.
What I have been too scared
to think of—
except in the cobwebby corners
óf my imagination—
is true.

No.
Don't say it.

Mom and Dad will not let anything bad happen.
But I remember Mom's pale face
as she snatched the letter.
I have to know what this all means.

I have to.

Mom and Dad are so busy
talking by the zucchini plant
in the vegetable garden
that they don't hear me coming.
Mom paces with Achilles on her hip.
"My family has been banking
at that bank for thirty-two years," she says.
"You'd think Charlie would have
the guts to come say this to our faces
instead of sending a form letter."

Dad, cutting a bat-size zucchini
from its stalk,
glances up and sees me.
"Claire," he says in a warning voice to Mom.
She turns,
sees me too,
and puts a smile on her face.
"Why, Eva," she says.

I open my mouth,
close it,
then open it again and say,
"I just Googled foreclosure."

Mom's smile fades.
Dad stands up with the zucchini in his hand.
"I'm sorry, honey," he says. "We didn't mean
for you to find out that way."
"So it's true?" I ask. "We're behind
on paying back the loan
to the bank?"

Mom and Dad both nod.

I try to swallow
but can't.
I try to speak
but can't.
Achilles stretches out his arms toward me,
and I take him from Mom.
With my face buried in his short brown curls
I say at last,
"What does all this mean?"

"It means," Mom explains,
that we could lose the Farm."

Everything seems to stop:
The wind stops blowing—
the birds in the blue spruce stop singing—

the river stops roaring—
the garden stops growing—
and the Farm itself
seems to heave a great sigh
because the words are out,
are spoken at last—
lose the Farm.

This farm has been in Mom's family
since Grandma Helen was a girl.
Mom grew up here.
I want to grow up here.
Achilles wants to grow up here too.
I hug him tight
against the ache in my chest.

Achilles reaches up,
pats my wet cheek,
and says, "Va."
Mom, Dad, and I all stare at him.
"What did you say, Achilles?" I ask.
"Did you try to say Eva?"
He beams. "Va!"
I cry harder.
Achilles has spoken his first word—
my name.

I whirl him around
again and again.
I will never lose Achilles.

First Word

Like a butterfly
from a cocoon,
the word
from his lips
changes
a baby
into
a brother.

Dad starts doing odd jobs—
when he can find them,
but they don't pay much.
Mom gets a new job,
waitressing in the Methow Café
on Thursday, Friday, and Saturday nights
to bring in more money.
That's all she can find.
And lucky to have it, she says,
because so many people
are out of work right now.

She says she will
write more articles,
but editors are picky,
she claims.
The truth is,
Mom hasn't sold one word—
not
one
word
since Grandma Helen died.

Me, I can't think of one thing
a twelve-year-old can do
to earn money.
So I feel pretty much worthless.
All I can do is look after Achilles
while Mom and Dad work.
But that doesn't bring in one cent,
unless Achilles starts pooping gold.

I leaf through my stack of poems,
written in my best chancery cursive calligraphy.
Poets are always poor—
unless they become poet laureates
or write greeting cards
or advertising slogans.

Maybe Dad is right.

Maybe I am wasting my time on poetry.

But I don't see how math or science

will save the Farm either.

I take out a blank sheet

of Canson calligraphy paper,

then hesitate.

Mom says when I use up

the last of my calligraphy paper,

there will be no money for more.

So I need to be sparing.

How can I be sparing with poetry?

Same Old Bear

Wood crackles the dawn,

and I know the same old bear is feasting

in the same old plum tree again.

Every year he swipes off whole branches,

gorging on glistening plums.

Does he dream of plundering our orchard

all winter in his stuffy den?

The tree looks worse every year—

mauled and broken—

but keeps bearing plums
as fat and red as a baby's cheeks.
The bear looks worse every year too—
muzzle gray, fur matted, one ear missing—
but keeps looting.

I keep expecting one of them to die—
the tree or the bear—
but they seem to need each other.
Which just goes to show you
that sometimes things work out fine
for everybody.
So long as that old bear
leaves a few plums for me.

Swinging in the hammock,
I look out over the orchard,
over the house with its shining metal roof,
over the tangle of the vegetable garden.
Does the Farm know
we might have to leave?
Could the land
help us stay?
I look the other way
and stare through the deer fence
at the wild canyon.

Is the Demon Snag
causing all our troubles?
Is it summoning
powerful evil magic
that creeps down the canyon
and slips through
the chimera of the deer fence?

The canyon and the Farm
must have kindly spirits as well.
I think of Mrs. Whatsit,
Mrs. Who, and Mrs. Which—
kindly spirits of stars—
who helped Meg become a heroine
and fight the darkness
and save her little brother.

How can I fight
the Demon Snag?
What kindly spirits will help
me save the Farm?

I decide to walk up the canyon alone
to confront the Demon Snag.
Then I picture the deer with its
bloody throat

lying slaughtered across the trail.
I have no magic,
I am not wearing my silver boots,
it is almost dark—
and I am not even brave enough
to go up alone in the light.
I slip out of the hammock,
trudge up to the Crow's Nest,
and fall asleep
with the skylight open.

Skylight at Night

Bats fly
like black ghosts
in and out
of the skylight
over my bed
at night.

Stars fly
like guardian angels
in and out
of the skylight
over my bed
at night.

Owls fly
like wizards
in and out
of the skylight
over my bed
at night.

Wishes fly
like whirling seeds
in and out
of the skylight
over my bed
at night.

Dreams fly
like magic carpets
in and out
of the skylight
over my bed
at night.

Sleeping deeply,
I remain.

The bank man
Mom calls Charlie

and I call Mr. Eyebrow
drives up our road this morning
to talk with Mom and Dad.

I don't like the look of Mr. Eyebrow.
In spite of the heat,
he wears a black suit
with a dark gray tie—
like an undertaker.
One black eyebrow
crawls across his forehead.
He is as tall and thin
as the Demon Snag.

Mom and Dad and Mr. Eyebrow
talk inside the house for a long time.
I sit on the deck
with Achilles
but can't hear a word.
Sirius curls beside us
as we watch heavy clouds gnaw the sky.

Achilles puts his hands on the railing
and pulls himself to his feet.
My hand hovers behind his back
in case he falls.

"We'll probably have to move to Seattle,
like Chloe did," I say to him.
"To some tiny horrible apartment.
You won't grow up knowing the Farm.
You won't know the orchard,
　　or harvest time,
　　or the deer,
　　or the old bear,
　　or the hammock,
　　or the gray squirrels,
　　or the garden,
　　or the sun daisies,
　　or Grandma Helen's haunted outhouse."

My stomach pushes
into my throat
until I almost throw up.
Grandma Helen never knew Achilles—
because she died
three months before he was born.
And now Achilles will never
really know Grandma Helen—
because he won't know the Farm.

Achilles crawls into my lap.
He senses something is wrong.

I grab his hand and kiss each fingertip
until he laughs.

When Mr. Eyebrow comes out of the house—
his shiny black shoes
shaking the deck with every step—
I clutch Achilles tight,
as though the man might steal him away too.
Achilles squirms.
Mr. Eyebrow doesn't say hi,
doesn't even look at us.
Dad walks out on the deck, softly,
and watches Mr. Eyebrow drive away
in his shiny red BMW.
"Well?" I ask.
"Get your rod," Dad says.
"We're all going fishing."
I cheer,
but Mom looks at Dad and sighs.

Fishing

I wait for a fish
from the deep
to rise

for my fly–
wait for something
from the deep
to rise
shining–
wait for anything
from the deep
to rise
to the light
and save us all.

On the way home from fishing,
we stop in Twisp for gas.
Through the truck window,
I watch people bustle around
the Twisp Farmer's Market,
buying and selling crafts and produce.
One kid sits at a card table
with a red plastic pitcher
and a stack of Styrofoam cups leaning
like the Tower of Pisa.
A sign printed in crooked black letters reads:
LEMONADE, 50 CENTS A CUP.
I wish I could sell something too,
to earn money.

But all I have are my poems.
No.
I could never show the world my poems.
Besides, who would want
to buy them?

After we come home,
after we eat four fat rainbow trout
fried in flour, salt, and pepper for dinner,
Dad and Mom call a family meeting
around the kitchen table.
Even Achilles attends,
banging his spoon on his high chair.
"We have three months," Mom says.
"Because we have been customers of the bank
for thirty-two years,
the bank is giving us
three extra months to catch up
before they start
foreclosure proceedings.
The Galas will bring in some money
when we pick them next month."
"But probably not enough," Dad says.
"We still need a miracle
in order to keep the Farm."

Farm Miracles

A miracle—
that apple blossoms
turn into fruit.

A miracle—
that birds learn to fly
without any lessons.

A miracle—
that sun daisies
bloom gold every spring.

A miracle—
that poems
rise out of the land.

A miracle—
is easy for the Farm.
A miracle for us to stay.

All night long I toss and turn
under the open skylight.
Can I,
dare I,
try to sell my poems?

Pull my secret heart
out of my chest
and lay it on the table for everyone to see?
I have to do something—
something to help save the Farm.
I would rather have someone
scorn my poems,
or worse,
laugh at them,
than lose the Farm.

In the morning I tell Mom and Dad
I want to sell my poems
at the Twisp Farmer's Market
next Saturday.
"Would a dollar a poem
be too much?" I ask.
"I think that sounds just right," Mom says.
But Dad says, "Don't get your hopes up
too high, Eva."

While I wish
I could sell copies of my poems
written on Canson calligraphy paper,
I don't have enough of that paper left.

So, over the next week,

I take the poems

I have already written out beautifully

and scan them into Dad's computer in the office.

Then I print out copies

on colored paper—

sky blue,

butter yellow,

sage green,

and petal pink.

Achilles crawls around my feet

while I work.

I pick him up and give him

a big kiss.

"Maybe," I tell him,

"I'll make enough money

from my poetry that you can grow up

on the Farm after all.

Maybe poems can make a miracle."

At the Twisp Farmer's Market

Apricots, apples, and artichokes,

carrots, cabbages, and crafts,

jewelry, jam, and jelly,

photographs of the Methow Valley—
tables and tables of treasures
at the Twisp Farmer's Market.

Sellers wait behind each table,
hoping the rich folks from Seattle
who have come to spend
the weekend in the country
will buy, buy, buy,
at the Twisp Farmer's Market.

I write that poem
sitting at my card table
waiting for customers.
Rocks hold down
the neat stacks of poems
to keep them from blowing away
in the wind.
Taped to the front of the table is a sign
Mom made on the computer:
A DOLLAR A POEM—SUPPORT YOUR LOCAL POET.

I am the only poet
at the market,
so there is no competition,
Mom says.

Dad lets me wear his baseball hat
for luck.

I half hope no one will stop.
But people do stop, smile,
and ask if I'm the poet.
I nod.
When they read my poems,
sweat blooms on my forehead,
and I want to slink under
the card table
and vanish.
For the Farm, I think,
gripping the seat of my metal folding chair.
For the Farm.

No one makes fun of me.
But every time someone reads a poem
and walks away without buying one—
sometimes without even a comment—
I droop like a wilted sun daisy.

Then a farmer in a blue-and-white-striped shirt,
who is selling vegetables
at the table next to me,
reads "Same Old Bear" three times.

He chuckles—in a nice way.

"Well, I'll be darned if I don't have a bear

just like that," he says. "But with me it's apricots

instead of plums. My wife

will get a kick out of your poem."

I stare at the dollar bill he hands me—

then smooth it through my fingers.

It is soft,

as though it has been through the wash

many times.

By noon, to my surprise,

I've sold all ten copies

of "The Haunted Outhouse,"

five copies of "Sprinklers,"

three copies of "Summer Storm,"

and six copies of "Same Old Bear."

By the end of the afternoon

I've made thirty-four dollars—

thirty-four dollars!

I proudly give it all to Mom and Dad.

They're surprised too,

especially Dad.

They give me back two dollars

to spend however I want.

I know exactly what I want.
I pass the candle maker's table
with its colorful pillars and tapers.
I pass the jam maker's table—
not even tempted
by the huckleberry preserves.
I pass belts,
pass fudge,
pass sausages,
pass lavender,
pass herbal wreaths,
pass inlaid boxes,
pass stained-glass windows.

At last
I reach the Bead Woman's table.
Mysterious and beautiful,
the Bead Woman wears scarves
in water colors.
A turquoise-blue scarf sparkling with crystals
circles her dark brown hair.
A cerulean-blue scarf
drapes around her neck.
A navy-blue scarf
wraps around her hips.
She makes jewelry with polished stone beads

in sober colors—
green, brown, rose, gold, white, black.
Some are round, some square,
some speckled.
Each bead is different, magical—
handmade
like a stone poem.
There are pendants, necklaces, bracelets, earrings—
exactly the kind of jewelry I imagine
a heroine would wear
as she battles powerful
Demon Snags in the wild canyon.

"Do you have anything for two dollars?" I ask.
The Bead Woman sadly shakes her head no,
her hair swinging
down to her waist.
"Would you trade a poem
for a bead?" I ask.
She smiles. "So you're the poet
everyone is talking about."
I blush to hear that people are talking
about me.
"You like rocks," I say.
"And I have a poem about a rock.
"Would you . . ." I take a deep breath.

"Would you like to read it?"

"I'd be honored," she says.

Canyon Rock

I found you,
rock,
your face glinting red
in the morning sunlight,
on the path
winding up the canyon.

I hold you,
your edges
declaring your
ancient journeys.

I take you,
who risked all dangers
the moment you were no more a mountain.
Take you
to shape you to my hand—
   as the wind did,
   as the rain and glacier did,
until you make of my heart, too,
an offering,

for someone walking by
who catches the morning sunlight on my face
and stops.

The Bead Woman gazes up at me,
gazes through to the center
of me—
gazes
and gazes
until I look down.
Then she reads my poem out loud
while I roll my two dollar bills
into a tight cylinder.
"This is enchanting!" she exclaims.
"You are a savant with words."
I ask, "What is a savant?"
She falls silent for a moment.
The sun sparks off the crystals
on the scarf in her hair,
and suddenly
she is crowned with a halo.
At last she says, "A savant is someone
with an extraordinary gift—
a gift that flows
directly from the great creative power
in the universe.

For this poem I will trade you
something special."

She reaches into a basket by her feet
in their gold leather sandals,
and pulls out a silver cord
with a rose-colored stone pendant
in the shape of a circle
dangling on the end.
I draw in my breath—
the polished stone looks like a sunrise
caught on a necklace.
A narrow band of green runs through it.
"This stone is called thulite," the Bead Woman says.
"It comes from right here in Eastern Washington
near Riverside.
The quarry is fiercely guarded
by rattlesnakes.
I give it to you
from one artist to another."

"Can it defeat evil spirits?" I ask.
The Bead Woman looks at me for a long time.
Then she says, "The power of the stone mirrors
the power of your own imagination."
Before I can ask her what she means,

another customer comes up—
a woman too dressed up
to be a local.
The Bead Woman gives me a little bow
and turns away.

When I slip the silver cord over my head,
the rose stone pendant
hangs over my heart.
I will wear it for the first day of school
on Monday.

Orchard Majesty

When I was little,
I asked Dad
why silver foil
sweeps down the rows
of apples like the
train of a queen.
Dad said—
Because the sun bouncing off the silver Mylar
reddens the apples.

When I was little,
I asked Dad
why red foil
decorates the tree branches
like crepe paper streamers
at my birthday party.
Dad said—
Because the red Mylar scares off the birds
who peck the apples.

When I was little,
I asked Dad

if the orchard
is getting ready for royalty,
because when the wind blows,
all the Mylar flashes and shimmers.
Dad said–
Maybe it is, because
after all, the pickers are coming soon.

As the weeks pass,
the apples grow
so big
and so heavy
upon the trees,
the branches begin to sag.
Dad and Mom
prop up the branches
with long sticks
to keep them
from breaking.

When the apples turn beautifully red,
turn perfectly ripe,
and turn the air so sweet
it is like living inside a flower,
harvest time swings around again.
Every year at harvest time

we have to find fruit pickers

to pick the apples and pears.

It gets harder every year.

Dad says it's because of government rules

about who can work where.

Picking fruit is hard

hard

hard

work.

Carrying a heavy bag

and climbing

up and down ladders

all day

in the scalding sun.

I am grateful for the fruit pickers.

Harvest Time

Feet creak
on shiny metal ladders
at Harvest Time.

Apples hug
in heavy pickers' bags
at Harvest Time.

Fruit bins stack
like LEGOs
at Harvest Time.

Tractors tango
down dusty roads
at Harvest Time.

Farmers worry
over next year's crop
at Harvest Time.

Two weeks after harvest,
I open my algebra book
in the Crow's Nest.
Ms. Spencer, my seventh-grade teacher,
assigned me extra algebra problems
for writing poems
during math class.
Dad would like her.
But she doesn't understand
that I must write new poems
to sell at the Twisp Farmer's Market
before it closes for winter.
I have repeat customers now,
asking what's new.

So I must keep writing poems.
Although I give Mom all the money,
she hasn't been giving any back lately.

After I've finished six problems,
I hear Mom and Dad arguing
down in the kitchen.
I perch at the top of the ladder
to listen.

"Maybe it wouldn't have come to this, Claire,"
Dad is saying, "if you'd spent more time
writing articles and less time
crying about Helen."
"You're blaming me?" Mom asks.
"Have you offered me any comfort
for losing my mother?
No! Not a shred.
You're too busy
saving the environment
to help your own wife."

Dad sighs. "I keep so busy
because I miss you."
"What do you mean?" Mom asks in a startled voice.
"When Helen died," Dad says,

"it was like you died too.
You went away from me.
I feel like I've lost my wife,
lost my best friend—to grief.
I'm lonely.
And now that we're facing this crisis,
I need you more than ever."

"I need you, too," Mom says softly.
"I didn't think things could get any worse.
But this latest news . . .
What are we going to do now?"

My heart lurches.
I climb down the ladder as fast as I can.
Mom and Dad stop talking
the instant I run into the kitchen.
"What's happened?" I ask.
"What's wrong?"

Mom is grim.
"The fruit company
that buys our fruit
didn't give us
the price we expected
for the Galas.

There won't be enough
money
to keep the bank from foreclosing
on the Farm."
Dad adds, "We'll have to sell the Farm
or lose everything."

"No!" I shout.
"You can't sell the Farm!
You can't!"
I snatch up Achilles.
He curls his fingers in my hair
as I run from the kitchen—
out of the house,
out into the orchard,
with Sirius following.

The apple branches arch over our heads
in a canopy of autumn gold.
I touch tree after tree.
Where is Pomona,
Roman goddess of orchards?
Where is Demeter,
Greek goddess of the land?
Where is Gaia,
great goddess of the earth?

I'm wild to pray,
wild to save the Farm
for Achilles—
and me.
And I do pray
to whatever god or goddess
might be listening.
But I think no one is.

A mist barrels down the canyon
and hovers over the Farm.
I imagine the Demon Snag
conjuring it, conjuring trouble.

With Achilles in my arms,
and Sirius by my side,
I roam through the orchard
until the full moon soars above the eastern hills
like a great white moth.
I remember how Grandma Helen
used to walk through the orchard
in her bare feet,
with her long silver hair
and me
floating behind her.

As the mist deepens,
I see a magical figure in my mind—
my Mrs. Whatsit—
the Apple Witch.

The Apple Witch

Leaves whirling
from her moonlit skirt,
the Apple Witch sings
to the orchard trees:
"Winter will pass.
Wait again for me!"

Blossoms flying
from her twig fingers,
the Apple Witch blesses
the orchard trees:
"Spring will come.
Wait again for me!"

All the next day in school
I wonder if the Apple Witch
can help me save the Farm.
Is she my magical helper?

Heroines always have one
in books and fairy tales.

In art class,
Mrs. Kramer has us make collages.
We're supposed to create
an autumn scene
with bits of torn paper
from catalogs
and old *National Geographic* magazines.
But I make a picture
of the Apple Witch instead.

Then Mrs. Kramer tells us about
Vision Boards.
A Vision Board is a big piece of poster board
that you fill with a collage
of words and pictures
from your imagination
to help make your dreams come true.

Could it work for me?
Could imagination help save the Farm?

After the school bus drops me off at home,
I trudge up our long dirt driveway,

past the Anjous,
past the Galas,
past the Haunted Outhouse,
until at last I reach the shed.
Metal rings against metal—
Mom is fixing the mower,
a wrench in her hand.

When I ask her for money
to buy a piece of poster board
to make a Vision Board,
she waves the wrench in the air.
"This blasted mower!" she exclaims.
"I swear it breaks down every week.
And there's no money for parts.
No money at all for parts,
and you're asking for poster board, Eva?"

My face grows hot.

Mom goes on. "I'm tired of broken equipment,
tired of irrigation pipes that always need fixing,
tired of fire blight,
hail,
drought,
bills,

and work that never ends.
I am tired of the Farm."

I can't say a word.
My heart grows so heavy
it needs a prop
to hold it up
and keep it from breaking.

"It's been like this my whole life, Eva,"
Mom adds. "Except when I was in college.
I want something more for you and Achilles.
Something better. Something special—"
"The Farm is special," I interrupt,
but she doesn't hear me.
"Maybe it's just as well," she says,
"that we're leaving this place behind."
Mom bends back to the mower.
The wrench clangs against a bolt.
"Have you picked those elderberries yet?" she asks.
"No? Then get to it. I want to make jelly."

I grab a bucket
and run out of the shed.
I can't believe

what I just heard.
I can't believe
Mom thinks the Farm
isn't special enough
for Achilles and me.

Elderberries

Purple berries
in the basket
will soon be jelly
on my toast.

But first—
we wash them
we steam them
we juice them
we add pectin
we stir in sugar
then boil
boil
boil
and fill jars
to open at
breakfast

so we can

eat summer

all winter long.

I write that poem on my last sheet

of Canson calligraphy paper,

write carefully

without blots

up in the Crow's Nest.

After Mom's outburst,

I'm afraid to ask for money

to buy more calligraphy paper.

So this will be the last Saturday

I sell new poems

at the Twisp Farmer's Market.

But it's closing soon for winter, anyway.

I type a long e-mail to Chloe,

even though I know she won't answer.

"The Farm is lost forever," I write at the end.

"How did you bear it?"

And hit send.

Words boil inside me

like the teakettle

when the water is whistling

for Mom's morning tea.
I am bubbling
with another poem
and no calligraphy paper
to write it on.
I could write
on lined school paper—
I could.
But I think a sheet of paper—
any paper—
is too small
for all that is inside me.

I need a Vision Board.

Fall light swoons
through the skylight.
I gaze at Heaven's Gate Mountain
beyond the deer fence,
up the canyon
where the Demon Snag
brews his terrible magic
to steal our Farm.
Now his terrible magic
has reached Mom's heart.

I touch the rose stone pendant

over my own heart—

the pendant the Bead Woman gave me.

I fill my pen with ink

and begin

to write poetry

BIG

HUGE

BEAUTIFUL

across the wall.

October Thief

I smell winter coming

on the cold wind

traipsing like a thief

from the Demon Snag

to steal my summer,

to steal my Farm.

Squirrels chitter

through the dry walnut leaves on the ground,

searching for nuts

they might have overlooked.

Oh, hoard, hoard

every bit of glory!
*   —every ray of sun*
*   —every cricket's chirp*
*   —every barefoot run across the grass*
before winter darkness lands
and the Farm is lost forever.

Three days pass
before Mom notices
the writing and pictures on my wall—
even though she has climbed
the ladder to the Crow's Nest
more than once.

When she finally notices,
her mouth falls open,
and her face frowns.
Then she sees the words I've written
in an arch
across the top of the wall
in my best calligraphy with flourishes:
SAVING THE FARM.
Her mouth shuts.

She reads the five poems about the Farm
I've written on the wall—

then runs her fingers
over the collaged pictures
I've made from old magazines and catalogs.
"That is Pomona," I say, pointing.
"That is Demeter.
And that is the Apple Witch—
I made her up.
I started with a little collage of her at school,
but she needed to be much, much bigger.
She reminds me of Grandma Helen."

Five feet high,
the Apple Witch opens her arms
in the center of the wall.
She has skin made of bark
that I peeled from an apple log.
A dress made of gold paper
that I tore from magazines.
Hair made of curling grapevines
that I cut into long strands.
"She's not finished yet," I tell Mom.
Here and there,
pictures of Achilles
that I printed out
dot the wall.

I've pasted letters on the wall too,
making words like—
    IMAGINATION
    MAGIC
    FIGHT
    WHATSIT
    WHEEL OF LIFE
    HEROINE
in all different colors.
I cut the letters
for the biggest word of all
from an old green apron
of Grandma Helen's—
    HOPE.

I tell Mom the wall is my Vision Board,
for saving the Farm.

"Oh, Eva," she says,
and sits down on my bed.
She puts her face in her hands and cries,
her brown hair falling forward
like two folded wings.

"Don't you like it?" I ask in a small voice.

"I've forgotten hope," she says,

"forgotten it."

She keeps crying.

Dad hears

and climbs up the ladder,

thinking it's me crying, I guess.

He sees Mom's tears,

sighs,

and then pats her shoulder once,

awkwardly.

When I take Mom's hand,

she squeezes it tight.

Then Dad notices the wall.

I explain how the collage I made at school,

and what Mrs. Kramer told us

about Vision Boards,

gave me the idea for the wall—

that and having no money

for calligraphy paper or poster board.

Dad doesn't say anything,

and I brace myself for another lecture

about poetry being a waste of time.

To my surprise,

he stares at the Apple Witch

and says at last,
"Hope is a powerful thing."
Which just goes to show you
that Dad has more imagination
than I thought.

"We have produced an artist," Mom says.
"You are like Michelangelo
painting on the ceiling
of the Sistine Chapel in Italy."

They don't make me paint over it.
They don't make me stop.
Mom tells me to keep going,
which, in my humble opinion,
is a wise thing to do.

Four-Wheeler

I zoom
the four-wheeler
between apple trees
lean, laugh, scream—
I'm going to fall!
But never do.

I wish life
were like this—
never falling,
daredevil, reckless
but safe
on four wheels.

Then I know—
Mom and Dad,
Achilles,
and Grandma Helen
are the four wheels
under me.

If I get stupid
or just unlucky
and fall,
they will pick me up
so I can go
roaring off again.

On Saturday afternoon
at the Twisp Farmer's Market,
a hot breeze denies
that winter is hurtling toward us.
I take a break from selling, on this,

my last day at the market,
and wander over to the Bead Woman's table.
A crowd surrounds her,
tourists just off a bus.
People finger the necklaces and stones
displayed on white ceramic trays
while the Bead Woman tries to talk
with everyone at once and make change, too.
A guy dressed all in black,
with red hair swinging
over his forehead,
slips a black pendant
into his pocket
and ambles away in his red Converse sneakers
without paying.
When he glances back over his shoulder
and sees me watching,
he smirks at my scalding frown.

My heart pounding,
I swallow hard,
but only glare at him,
too afraid to say a word.

I walk around to the back
of the Bead Woman's table

and stand beside her
under the blue-fringed umbrella
that shades her
from the sun.
She looks up at me from her chair.
"Why, Eva. Good afternoon," she says, surprised,
then turns back to a woman
in a spotless white eyelet dress
who is buying an expensive necklace
and matching earrings
made of blue and green stones
that remind me of a river bottom.

Standing as still and alert as a fishing heron,
I watch everyone,
make sure they see me watching them.
Nobody else steals anything.
I stand guard for almost an hour
until the tourists get back on the bus
and ride away.

The Bead Woman turns to me at last
with a question in her dark eyes.
"I saw . . . ," I begin. "I saw
a guy steal one of your pendants.
I didn't want that to happen again,

so I stood guard."
The Bead Woman smiles. "What a comfort
to know a guardian angel
is looking out for me. Thank you.
Let me pay you for the hour you spent."
But I shake my head. "That's all right.
We sellers have to look out
for each other."
I give her a shy smile.

"I see you're wearing your thulite pendant,"
the Bead Woman says
as she stands and stretches—
as though she might be a dancer.
"I wear it all the time," I say.
She nods. "No wonder the stone has changed."
"Changed how?" I ask.
"Stones become glossier
after they're worn. They take on
something of your own spirit and power."

The Bead Woman's gold skirt swirls
as she sits down again.
Today she wears all gold—
a gold silk scarf in her hair,
a gold cotton peasant blouse,

the calf-length gold skirt.
Her skin is the color of dark honey.
I wonder how old she is.
No older than my mom,
I guess.

I ask, "How do you know
how to arrange the stones
in such beautiful patterns
in the necklaces?"
"The stone tells the necklace," she says.
"What I mean is,
if you look carefully enough,
the stone will reveal—
through its color, its shape, its texture—
what kind of necklace it wants to be.
Especially the pendants."

I think about this.
"My best poetry is the same," I say.
"If I listen hard enough, the poem tells me
what it wants to be while I'm shaping it."
"Exactly," says the Bead Woman.
"So how do you shape stones?" I ask.
"Well, I start by cutting them on a lapidary saw,
then . . ." She stops. "Ah—I am graced

with an idea. Why don't we ask
your parents to bring you
to see my workshop?"
My jaw falls open. "Really?" I ask.
She smiles. "Really."

The very next day
Mom drives me to the Bead Woman's house—
she lives just north of Carleton,
between us and Twisp.
Flowers circle her house
like the skirt on a ballerina.
Tall, tangled flowers
leap one over the other.
I know all their names
because Chloe taught me:
    —purple asters,
    —pink coneflowers,
    —gold chrysanthemums,
    —pink, white, and lavender phlox
      that smell like heaven.
Curving rock walls wind
between the flower beds.

"I like your garden," I tell the Bead Woman
when she walks out to greet us.

She laughs. "My glorious jungle!
It's in desperate need of weeding
and general fall cleanup.
Come along with me,
and I'll show you
my workshop out back."

A stream twines through her backyard—
a joyful, bubbling stream,
chattering and cajoling
through the listening
pine trees and flowers.

Animal bones bleached white by the sun—
skulls, backbones, whole spines—
cover the workshop's outer wall
in beautiful patterns.
I am struck, and stand looking,
surprised that anyone would use
bones
for decoration—
would see the beauty in
bones—
would want
this reminder

of death

so near.

Inside the workshop,

mismatched mason jars

full of rough beads

in a jumble of colors

crowd every windowsill.

Rocks cut in half

show off their inner color.

Mom admires a violet-colored one.

"That is charoite," the Bead Woman says.

"It helps with courage and imagination.

The one beside it is Madagascar jasper—

excellent for protecting and nurturing."

A brilliant, speckled blue stone catches my eye.

"What's this one called?" I ask,

putting my hands behind my back

because I'm so tempted to touch the stone.

The Bead Woman says, "That one is Parrot Wing

or chrysocolla. Good for unconditional love.

Go ahead and touch the stones," she adds,

as if she knew what I was thinking.

The Bead Woman shows us

her lapidary machine

with its saws and wheels
for cutting, shaping, and polishing
the stone.
"Water runs over everything while I work,"
she explains, "to cool the machinery.
The whole process is water based—
and quite messy."
She looks at me. "But don't you often find
that you have to make a mess
on the path
to making something beautiful?"

I'm not sure how to answer that,
but I like the question.
I hear the stream
through the flung-open windows,
and I'm not surprised that water
flows through
everything the Bead Woman does.

"It takes days to make
enough beads for a necklace,"
the Bead Woman says.
She sees me looking
at the dusty jars of beads.

"Someday I will get around to sorting
those by color and size," she says.
"That would make it much easier
to create the necklaces."

I say, "You could certainly use
some help around here."
"Eva!" Mom exclaims.
But the Bead Woman only laughs.
"You're absolutely right!"
She considers me gravely.
"How would you like a part-time job?" she asks.
My heart lifts,
and I want to jump up and down
like a five-year-old.
"You mean it?" I ask.
"I do. To start,
you could clean up my garden.
Then, when the weather turns cold,
you could sort and organize beads and tools.
There's a lot here that needs doing."

I look at Mom,
who has a considering look on her face.
"What a wonderful opportunity for Eva," she says.

"But I'll need to talk it over
with her father, of course."
"Certainly," says the Bead Woman.

I know I will plead,
beg,
argue,
fight—
do anything to get my parents to say yes.
Not just to earn money,
but to be around the Bead Woman
in this place
of water,
flowers,
creation,
life—
that feels somehow
holy.

That night,
Mom and Dad talk over
the Bead Woman's offer.
Mom makes several calls to friends
who know the Bead Woman well.
"Everything checks out, Eva,"
Mom says when she hangs up

after the last call.
"So you have yourself a job.
But you must promise
to keep up your grades
and your chores around here."
"I promise!" I exclaim.

After school on Friday,
Mom drops me off
at the Bead Woman's house
for my first afternoon of work.
The Bead Woman asks,
"Would you like to start
by weeding the jungle?"
"Sure," I say.
She gives me gloves and gardening tools.
I go right to work pulling weeds
by the stream,
which constantly has something to say,
keeping me company.

Now and then, I glance up at the bones
on the workshop wall.
I think about the dead deer in the canyon
at home.
I think about magical places,

like this place and the Farm.
I think about all the mysterious pieces
that come together
to make magical places.
And for the first time I wonder
if I could make
a new magical place for myself,
if we lose the Farm.

When the Bead Woman brings me
a glass of pink lemonade,
I'm surprised that two hours have passed.
The lemonade tastes sparkly on my tongue.
"You don't have any fences here," I say.
She nods. "I don't have vegetables,
so I've never needed a fence.
And I like seeing what will wander in—
mostly deer.
Though I'm always hoping for dragons!"
She smiles.

She has a wild imagination too!
I knew it!
I could tell by this place
and by the necklaces she makes.
The Bead Woman picks a purple aster

and tucks it behind my ear.

"I cultivate a wild imagination," she says,

as if she knows what I'm thinking.

I say, "My dad says I have too much imagination

for my own good. I'm not allowed

to watch horror movies

because I imagine all kinds of terrible things."

The Bead Woman shakes her head.

"It is impossible

to have too much imagination.

You simply have to learn how

to shape it,

to tame it, and especially,

to call it to your hand.

Learn to conjure angels instead of monsters."

I say, "Sometimes you don't have to conjure monsters.

They're just there."

"What do you mean?" she asks.

"I mean coyotes, bears, and cougars.

And the biggest monster of all—

the bank."

She sees me shiver and says,

"Sometimes we face our fears

in the most unexpected places.

Then imagination can help us,

because it is one of the Greater Powers."

"One of the Greater Powers?" I ask.

"You mean power like magic?"

"Yes, imagination is magical.

It certainly has transforming properties."

I take another sip of lemonade, then ask,

"What are the other Greater Powers?"

"Love, hope, and joy," she says.

Hope.

I think of Mom,

who said she has forgotten hope,

and at that moment hear

the truck pull up,

the tires crunching on the gravel road.

The Bead Woman rises.

"That must be your mom coming to pick you up."

I look at the garden.

I've barely made a dent in the weeds.

Although I don't want to leave yet,

I get up too.

The weeks pass quickly,

filled

with school,

with babysitting Achilles,
with writing poems and making pictures
on the wall in the Crow's Nest,
and best of all,
with working for the Bead Woman.
But I never forget,
never,
that we may lose the Farm.

Thanksgiving comes at last.

During Thanksgiving dinner
we have a tradition.
We go around the table
and each say what we are thankful for.
Dad says, "I'm thankful
for all of you,"
as he does every year.
"What are you thankful for, Achilles?" I ask.
In his high chair,
Achilles bangs his sippy cup against the tray
and says, "Eat!"
We laugh.
I finger my rose stone pendant.
"I'm thankful," I say, "for two things.
First, that we are still at the Farm.

Second, that I have a job
with the Bead Woman."

Mom doesn't say anything.

So we wait—
the turkey steaming,
the smell of sausage stuffing
making me want to stuff myself
until I'm as fat as the turkey.

At last Mom reaches into her shirt pocket
and pulls out a slip of pale green paper.
"I'm thankful for this," she says.
"I sold Grandma Helen's watch,
and this is the check."
As she waves it,
I see lots of zeros.
My heart rises and sinks
in the same breath.

"Oh, Claire," Dad murmurs to Mom.

I say, "How could you sell
Grandma Helen's watch?
That's like selling a piece of our family."

Mom says, "It was a hard decision.
But I think Grandma Helen would approve.
This land was more important to her than any watch."
I grip my plate,
blue willow china—
Grandma's Helen's wedding china
that we use only on holidays.
"That watch was mine, too," I say.
"And you didn't even ask me
about selling it."
Mom stabs the fork in the turkey.
"Don't make this harder than it is, Eva."
She starts carving.

Not hungry anymore,
my stomach feels as heavy as an anchor
at the bottom of a lake.
I ask, "Did you at least
get enough money for the watch
to save the Farm?"
Mom says there is enough money
to give us three more months
before we have to sell the Farm.
"And anything could happen
between now and then," Dad adds cheerfully,
"anything. Now, let's eat!"

But I look at Mom's wrist.
She always wears Grandma Helen's watch
for special occasions—
except for my birthday,
when I get to wear it.
But Mom's wrist is bare now,
and now, on my birthday, mine will be too.

How much more
will be lost?
How much wider
will the ragged hole
in my chest grow?
    First Grandma Helen,
    then Chloe,
    then the pears,
    now the watch,
    and maybe even . . .

No.
I
won't
think
it.

Old Man Woodstove

Old Man Woodstove
chortles and snorts
belching heat
from his hot full belly
that steams wet mittens
hanging on hooks—
that steams the wet dog
snoring on the rug—
that steams wet me
bringing in more wood
from the snow
to stuff in his greedy belly
that keeps us warm
all winter long.

The end of the Farm
begins with crying in the winter night.
Achilles.
Then coughing.
Achilles.
Then a fever of 103 degrees.
Achilles.

Then Mom and Dad and me
rushing off to the hospital
in Brewster.
Then Achilles flying
over the snowy Cascade Mountains
in a special plane with Mom
to Children's Hospital in Seattle.

Oh, Achilles.

Lost
I find a nest
fallen from
the maple tree
where the robin
used to sing.

An empty nest
blown down by
the North Wind
where the robin
used to sing.

Bits of broken
blue shell

cling to the nest
where the robin
used to sing.

Dad and I drive through the steep darkness
for five hours
over two treacherous mountain passes
to catch up to Mom and Achilles
in the hospital in Seattle.
In the passenger seat of the truck,
I lie awake under a wool blanket,
watching
fat flakes of snow
smash against the dark window—
listening
to the click of the windshield wipers,
which seem to chant
streptococcus pneumonia
streptococcus pneumonia
over
and over
and over
until the words are beaten into my brain.
How can Achilles
fight something he can't even say?
Weary, we stagger

into the hospital at last,
and find Mom huddled over Achilles's bed
in the intensive care unit.
So many tubes stick out of him
he looks like an alien creature
from a science fiction movie,
a very pale alien creature
whose beautiful blue eyes are shut.
Even with the oxygen tube
his nostrils flare,
and his chest sinks
as he struggles to breathe.
Mom tells us the doctors think
he has something called sepsis—
a life-threatening complication
of streptococcus pneumonia.

"Don't die, Achilles," I whisper.
"Don't leave us like Grandma Helen did."
I can't bear it,
cannot
bear
to lose
Achilles, too—
to have him be no more
than a memory—

to have the hole in my chest
rip
beyond
imagining.

Mom grips my shoulder
as hot tears glide down my face.
Dad grasps Mom's shoulder,
and she places her hand over his.
They stand looking at each other,
looking and looking.
Then they are hugging,
hugging and crying.
I have not seen them hug in a long time.
Soon the nurse shoos us out
to the waiting room,
where I try to sleep on a couch.
Breathe, Achilles, I think,
breathe.

At last I do sleep.
Now and then I wake up
to see Mom and Dad drinking coffee
and speaking quietly together—
holding hands.
I wonder how close Chloe lives to the hospital—

when she will come.

In the afternoon,

Mom calls Mrs. Quetzal, Chloe's mom.

They talk for a few minutes,

then Mom hands me the phone.

Mrs. Quetzal says,

"Hello Eva. I'm so sorry

to hear about Achilles. I'll put Chloe on."

I hear the sound of muffled arguing.

At last I hear Chloe's voice.

"I'm sorry to hear about Achilles,"

she echoes her mom.

"Thanks," I say. "Did you get all my e-mails?"

Chloe says, "I guess so. I've been pretty busy.

You know. School and friends and stuff."

I ask, "Can you come to see us at the hospital?"

"No. My mom doesn't want me near any germs."

"Oh," I say.

The silence stretches out like gum.

"Well," Chloe stammers, "I've got to go now."

"Wait!" I exclaim, because I have so much more

to say. "I miss you. And Camp Laughing Waters . . ."

but she has already hung up.

A doctor pads by in her white coat

and sneakers.

Can she stitch up
the ragged hole in my chest?

We stay at the hospital for three days.
During that time,
they only let me see Achilles once more.
"You are the greatest of Greek heroes, Achilles,"
I tell him. "Fight hard."
I will the red line on his heart monitor
to keep moving.
I will his chest
to keep rising and falling.

The Greek hero Achilles's mom
dipped him in the River Styx
so he would be invincible—
all but the heel where she held him.
I wish Mom had dipped our Achilles
in the Methow River
so he would be invincible too.

Finally we check into a motel,
because we all need showers,
but either Mom or Dad always
stays at the hospital with Achilles.
I sleep in a real bed,

but dream of the Demon Snag

holding his black ball—

evil shooting out like lightning.

At dawn I wake

to the sound of Dad's cell phone ringing.

He grabs it,

and I can tell he is talking to Mom.

Then Dad turns to me with a big grin and shouts,

"Achilles's fever is down!

It's down!

He's still very sick,

but with time and care,

the doctors believe he'll make it.

He'll pull through, Eva!"

Whooping, I jump out of bed,

throw my arms around Dad,

and then dance around the motel room

in my yellow cat pajamas.

I open the worn curtains to see a pink sky,

imagine Aurora—

rosy-fingered goddess of the morning—

and think of the Greater Power of Hope.

It is a new day,

a day Achilles is going to see.

The next morning
Dad and I drive back to the Farm,
because Mom and Dad don't want me to miss
any more school.
When we get home,
I tramp all over the orchard in my silver boots,
while Sirius barks
and brings me his Frisbee to throw.
The neighbors took good care of him
while we were gone,
but I bet they didn't throw his Frisbee
nearly enough.

Snow Angels for Achilles

Sit
in the pure snow.

Fall
on your back.

Swish
arms up and down.

Make
a snow angel.

Do
it again.

Fill
the orchard with angels.

Watch
them rise from the snow.

Send
them flying to Achilles.

"Dad! Dad!" I cry,
when I come in all crusted with snow
and pull off my blue hat.
"I sent a hundred snow angels
to Achilles!"
"That's fine, Eva," Dad says,
sitting at the kitchen table.
But his face looks serious.
"Sit down," he adds.
"There is something you should know."
My grin fades.
I can't breathe,
and my fingers crush my hat.
I don't sit down.

"Is it Achilles?" I ask quickly.

"Is he . . . worse again?"

"No, no," Dad assures me.

"Achilles is going to be fine.

But there are new expenses, Eva."

"What do you mean?" I ask.

"Medical bills," Dad says,

"bills, bills, and more bills.

For the hospital,

the doctors, the tests, and the special plane."

"But," I protest,

"we have medical insurance.

You and Mom are always complaining

about how much it costs."

Dad sighs. "Our insurance will pay

some of the bills,

but not everything.

Not nearly enough."

My heart shrinks.

I ask, "Will this eat up all the money

from Grandma Helen's watch?"

Dad nods. "And then some.

I am afraid we must

put the Farm up for sale."

I back away from him,
back away
and away,
shaking my head.
"There must be something," I begin,
my voice a squeak. "Something—"
"No," Dad says. "There is nothing we can do.
We're out of options.
I'm so sorry, Eva."

I bolt across the room,
fling open the front door,
and run outside.
The snow angels I made for Achilles—
all white and clean and perfect—
glitter
in the sunlight,
taunt
in the winter silence.

"I won't leave!" I scream,
and jump onto a snow angel.

I stomp the angel's wings,
smash its head,

crush its skirt.
As I kick and tramp,
grass and dirt fly up,
mixing with the snow,
turning it ugly.

Everything is silver—
the snow flying,
my breath streaming,
my boots kicking.

I run to the next snow angel
and wreck it, too,
then run to the next
and the next,
until nothing is left
but silver tears
falling on
ugliness.

Always Winter

Yellow school buses squirt
down the snowy road
like Twinkies on wheels.

I wait for mine to gobble me up—
wait beside the "For Sale" sign
swinging in the wind.

I want to stay home on the orchard
instead of sitting
packed like a sardine in school.
I want summer—
    crickets rampaging
    hammock swinging
    skylight shining
    fish biting.

My bus screeches to a stop
to pick me up.
I stomp up the steps
into a stink like the inside
of an old man's boot.

Through the steamy window
I see Dad pruning the apple trees.
See scraggly branches
littering the snow like giant antlers—
and know that it is still winter
and probably always will be—
because there will never be

another summer
at the Farm—
because I will no longer be
Eva of the Farm.

On a gray Christmas Day—
   without a tree
   without a turkey
   without Grandma Helen's watch
   without Mom
   without Achilles,
Dad gives me a tiny blue journal
to write poems in.
I'm surprised,
but guess that Mom picked it out.
I thank him,
even though the journal is too small.
It's the same periwinkle blue
as the sheet over Grandma Helen's
broken spinning wheel in the shed.

When I see the Bead Woman again,
she gives me a Christmas gift too—
a hummingbird's nest.
Inside is a delicate bird skull
and a tiny polished stone egg

that she made.
I put it all away in my closet—
I don't want it too close,
scared I might dream
of death.

Now that winter has come,
I work inside the Bead Woman's workshop,
sorting beads,
dusting,
and organizing shelves of tools and supplies.
Sometimes we talk while we work.
Today, though, the Bead Woman
has hardly spoken a word.
I wonder if I've done something wrong.
She sends me
into the house for a jar of beads
on the coffee table in her living room.
It's the first time I've been inside
her house.

I enter through the kitchen door
and smell freshly baked bread.
Bunches of dried herbs—
rosemary, basil, and sage—
hang from the ceiling.

In the living room,
a big piano
reigns like a queen.
A fringed blue cloth drapes over the lid,
which is covered with pictures.
I step closer to look at them.

In one picture, a golden-haired girl
plays with rocks
by a crumbling birdbath in a garden.
In another picture, the same girl
sits on a log in pink-and-white-striped pajamas,
surrounded by sun daisies.
Many of the pictures show the Bead Woman
and the little girl together.
In no picture
is she older than five or six.
I wonder who she is,
where she is,
then suddenly feel guilty for looking.
So I pick up the jar of beads.
I turn to go, but stop.

Hanging grandly framed on the wall
is my poem "Canyon Rock,"
which I gave to the Bead Woman

in exchange for my rose stone pendant.
I blink in surprise,
then go back outside
and cross the sleeping garden.

On the peak of the workshop roof,
the weathervane turns
in the fitful breeze—
copper coyotes
chasing a copper moon.

The Bead Woman sits
staring out the window
at the stream.
Though silenced by ice,
the stream is still beautiful,
sparkling in the sun.
I hand her the jar.
"Thank you," the Bead Woman says.
She threads one bead onto a leather cord,
sighs, and puts down the half-made necklace.
"Is something wrong?" I ask.
"Only sadness," she says.
She looks at me, hesitates, then adds,
"My only child, my daughter, Garnetta,
was taken from me five years ago today."

I think of the pictures on the piano.
Achilles flits into my mind,
but I push him out.
"Taken from you?" I ask. "What do you mean?"
"Garnetta was kidnapped
when she was six years old."

Shocked, my fingers freeze
on the stone beads.
I cannot
imagine
being taken from Mom and Dad.
I don't want to imagine it.
"That's awful!" I blurt. "I mean, I'm so sorry."

The Bead Woman shakes her head.
"You were right the first time.
"It is awful. But over the years I've learned
to change my thoughts away from awfulness.
I work hard to imagine
she's with a loving family
that really needed her.
I imagine what she might be doing—
going to school,
playing,
sleeping in a bed with a pink quilt—

pink was her favorite color.
But some days, like today,
are more difficult than others."

I think how imagination can
both torment and comfort us.
How it is one of the Greater Powers
along with hope.
I know how hard it is to stay hopeful—
since Achilles got sick,
I've had little hope for the Farm.
"Do you still hope?" I ask.
"Hope that she'll be found?"

The Bead Woman opens the glass door
on the woodstove,
puts on another log,
and pumps air into the flickering coals.
"I hope that Garnetta is happy.
I hope that she is well.
I hope that she is loved.
I hope she has an imagination as wondrous
as yours."
A flame licks up the wood.
"Ah," the Bead Woman adds, smiling,
"I think I know what to do

with this necklace now.
What would you think of all white stones?
Like the garden in winter?"

When I leave that day,
I give the Bead Woman a hug.
She stands in front of her house,
arms wrapped around herself
against the cold,
then waves
as I drive away with Dad—
so happy to be with Dad
and not kidnapped with some stranger.

Two weeks later,
when Achilles at last comes home
from the hospital with Mom,
I can't look at him.
He almost died,
and
I
can't
look
at
him.

In the blue journal,
I scribble the tiniest poem ever—
a poem I don't want anyone
ever
to see.

Hate
Ripped
from the Farm
like an uprooted tree
that hates
the wind—
I hate you.

I take the blue journal
and throw it
into the hole
in Grandma Helen's
haunted outhouse.
Then I run through
every row
in the pear orchard—
faster and faster—
until I reach the wind machine
at the heart.

A tall electric windmill
that spins around and around,
the wind machine keeps
the pear blossoms warm
during the frosts of spring.
Grandma Helen loved the roar of it—
"It sounds like hope,"
she used to say.
I lean my forehead against the metal.
It is cold
cold
cold—
unmoving,
powerless,
hopeless
in the still silence of winter.

My face is tight
and hot with tears.
I look up at the sky,
but no poem comes,
no comfort comes.
I throw my arms around
the wind machine and sob.
What if I can't write poems
once we leave the Farm?

What if sadness stops me,
the way it has Mom?

I stand,
listening to the trees
until my tears stop—
quietly listening to the trees
until their branches reach down
and give me a poem.

Leaves Longing

Without leaves,
the pear trees
look like candelabras
with silver arms.

The leaves huddle
on the ground,
rattling when the wind blows,
like an old man with a cough.
Do the leaves long
for their old homes?
Long to be back up high
where they could see forever?

When we leave
the Farm,
I will never stop longing
to get back.

Evangeline in the old poem
had to leave
her farm in Acadia, too,
forced out by the king of England.
She wandered across America
looking for her lost love, Gabriel,
until she was old
and finally found him again
just before he died.
Will we wander too?
The Farm lost forever?
How can Mom want that?

Hear Me!
I press my rose stone pendant
against the maple trees that hold
the hammock in summer.
"Save the Farm," I whisper.
But the space between the trees is empty,
as though part of me has already been erased

from the Farm.
They cannot hear me.

I circle my rose stone pendant
around the Gala trees
and the Anjou trees
in the orchard.
"Save the Farm," I call.
But the trees are bare now in winter,
sleeping.
They cannot hear me.

I swing my rose stone pendant
through the dried leaves
of the sun daisies that speckle
the south hill with gold in spring.
"Save the Farm," I cry.
The leaves clack
like bones in the wind.
They cannot hear me.

I dip my rose stone pendant
into the Methow River,
which winds like a blue memory
beside the road.

"Save the Farm!" I shout.
But the river only groans
of ice.
It cannot hear me.

The land has no power in winter.
Only the power of rest and sleep and dreaming.

A few people see the horrid FOR SALE sign
and come with the horrid real estate agent,
Mrs. Jared,
to poke around the Farm.
I follow them everywhere,
pointing out flaws—
    the woodpecker holes in the house,
    the corner of the orchard that sometimes freezes,
    the rickety spray shed—
until Mrs. Jared speaks to Mom.
"Stop bothering folks," Mom tells me,
embarrassing me right in front of Mrs. Jared,
who wears gold hoop earrings
big enough to punch a fist through.
"If you don't," Mom adds,
"we'll never sell this place."

"You don't even care, do you?" I shout.
"You don't care if we lose the Farm!
Grandma Helen would hate you!"

I run into the house,
slam the door,
and storm up the ladder to the Crow's Nest,
where I throw myself on my bed.
Horrid Mrs. Jared has also hinted
the house would look better
without the "mess"—
what she calls my Vision Board on the wall.
So far Mom and Dad have ignored this,
to my relief.

As the weeks pass
and winter deepens,
no one offers to buy the Farm.
I'm glad,
though Mom and Dad
look more worried every day.
Dad says the real estate market is poor
because there are too many places for sale.
Nobody wants to buy right now
because the economy is so bad.

"If nobody buys the Farm," I ask,
"can we stay?"
"No," Dad says.
"The bank will take everything,
and we will not have a cent to start over
somewhere else."

I don't want to start over somewhere else.

I wander outside
and stand at the deer fence,
looking up the wild canyon.
It is the Demon Snag's fault
that Achilles got sick—
the Demon Snag's fault
that Mom doesn't care—
the Demon Snag's fault
that we're going to lose the Farm.

I shake the fence,
shake it,
shake it,
until the wire leaves red marks
on my palms.
It is the deer fence's fault too,

for not being strong enough
to keep out the powers of darkness,
for being a chimera.
But most of all it is my fault
for being too scared to go up the canyon
to fight the Demon Snag.

I slink back into the house
and stare at Achilles in his crib.
Though purple shadows linger
like tiny cobwebs under his eyes,
he is better now.
His shirt with the yellow duck hangs on him—
the duck looks crumpled.
He reaches out his thin arms for me—
arms that used to be chubby—
and grins his lopsided grin.
I walk away,
ignoring his cries of "Va! Va!"
as Dad used to ignore Mom
when she cried for Grandma Helen.

Up in the Crow's Nest,
I kneel beside the stack
of magazines and catalogs
that I use to make the pictures

on my Vision Board wall.
I flip through an old *National Geographic*,
stop at a picture of the night sky
without stars—
without a moon—
a black night sky.

I rip it out.
I smear the back
with glue,
jump up,
and slap the black sky
over one of Achilles's pictures
on the wall.
Glee snags my heart
as I stand looking,
stand nodding my head, yes.
A fierce howling wind
fills me.
I reach for another magazine—
tear blackness
rip
storm
paste—
yes
yes
yes!

Outside the skylight,
a woodpecker drums the house.
I pound the wall back,
screaming, "Leave us alone!"

Owl on a Stick

Outside, woodpeckers drum
holes all over the house.
Mom puts up a twelve-foot pole
with a fake black owl on top.
"We are now worshippers of Athena,"
she says, laughing. "Greek goddess of owls."
She hopes the black owl will scare
away the woodpeckers.

But that very afternoon
I see a woodpecker tapping
a hole in the owl's eye,
searching for God—
like me.

The gods aren't listening.
I must defeat the Demon Snag
alone—

as Joan of Arc would
or Meg would.

But I'm scared.
Which is worse, I ask myself
day after day,
getting eaten by a cougar or bear
or losing the Farm?
Why do I have to make such
a terrible choice?

One gloomy afternoon,
I read everything I've written
on the Crow's Nest wall,
and look at every picture.
The Apple Witch—
her grapevine hair curling—
seems to whisper to me:
    Dreaming is not enough.
    You have to act
    to make your dream come true.

I break off a piece of grapevine
and weave it in my braid.
I pull on my silver boots

from the thrift shop.
I polish my rose stone pendant
from the Bead Woman.
A minute later,
I stand in front of the gate
in the deer fence
that leads to the wild canyon.
In the gloomy afternoon light,
the snow lolls like a hungry gray tongue.

I stand at the gate for a long time,
getting colder and colder.
When at last I put out my hand
to lift the latch,
a coyote howls.
Another coyote answers,
then another,
and another,
until the whole pack is wailing,
until the whole canyon is wailing,
until the whole world is wailing.

My blood races.
The coyotes are close.
Did the Demon Snag send them?
I turn away from the gate,

my shoulders slumped.

Back inside the house,
I see Achilles take two tottering steps
away from Dad
and into Mom's outstretched arms.
My mouth falls open in surprise.
When did Achilles start walking?
"I can't imagine," Dad says to Mom
in a muffled voice, "if we had lost him. . . .
I understand now about Helen.
Why you were so . . .
devastated.
I'm sorry."
Mom kisses Dad on the forehead.

Then they notice me.

Dad smiles and pushes up his glasses.
"Do you want to help
your brother learn to walk?"
I shake my head.
"It's not his fault, Eva," Mom says softly.
I don't say anything.
Dad says, "I'm sure Achilles would love
for you to build him a castle—"

"He would just ruin it," I interrupt,
"like he does everything."
I climb up to the Crow's Nest
alone.

"You are quiet today, Eva," the Bead Woman says
the next Saturday afternoon.
I am threading pairs of beads
onto a leather cord.
I put the cord down. "I'm having trouble
with my imagination."
"Tell me," she says.
I hesitate—
too shy to tell her
about the Apple Witch and the Demon Snag.
Instead I say, "I'm afraid of the wild canyon
behind the Farm.
I keep imagining
what claws and teeth can do.
So I'm afraid to go up there alone,
even though I need to.
I really, really need to. . . ."

The Bead Woman stands.
"Call your mom
and ask if you can stay late tonight.

I'll drive you home."
"What are we going to do?" I ask.
"It's a mystery," she says.
"You mean it's a secret?"
"No, I mean it is a mystery."

An hour later,
swaddled in coats and hats,
we follow a well-trodden path
in the snow
up over the hill
above the Bead Woman's house.
Behind it is another hill,
and we climb that one too,
only to see a third hill,
then a fourth—
seemingly endless hills
rising in waves
to the feet of the snowbound mountains
northward.

Twilight grazes the sky.

After we climb one last hill—
winding around rocks and snowy clumps
of bitterbrush—

we come to a canyon,

not my canyon,

not so beautiful,

but just as wild,

and somber with pines

clinging to stone cliffs

with their roots

exposed.

As the day fades

into stillness,

we walk

until we reach a clearing

in the canyon.

The Bead Woman pulls off her gloves

and digs down through the snow

until she finds a piece of grass.

The lip of the full moon,

rising yellow,

crowns the eastern hill.

I wonder why we are here.

The Bead Woman kneels

behind a bush

and motions for me to kneel
beside her—
as though we are in a cathedral
of winter.
She arranges the piece of grass
between her thumbs
and . . . blows.

A cry blasts out,
a shrieking,
a wailing,
a gasping after life being lost.
As it tears through my heart,
I think of the Bead Woman's lost daughter,
Garnetta,
think of the Farm,
about to be lost too.
When the Bead Woman pauses,
my ears ring in the sudden silence.
Then she repeats the cry—
enlightening the hills
with grief,
with a last struggle
as the pines bear witness.
Again she stops.

"What . . . ?" I begin.

The Bead Woman places one finger

against her lips.

"Wait and watch," she whispers,

looking out at the hills

that seem to be alive now,

that seem to be watching us in turn.

I hear a crackle,

a drumming,

and then I see them:

silvery-gray shapes

coming

down from the hills—

coyotes

running across the snow—

five coyotes

coming

straight toward us.

I want to run,

but the Bead Woman puts a hand

on my arm.

The coyotes keep

coming.

They are beautiful,
magical,
gods of the wild.
My heart pounds so loudly
I think they must hear it,
must seek
to devour it.
I am afraid.
I am enchanted.

Closer and closer
they come,
like silver water
pouring down the canyon.

"Now," the Bead Woman whispers,
"Stand up."
We rise.

The coyotes see us.
Without thought,
without missing a stride,
they veer,
scattering,

then vanish into the hills
and are gone
as suddenly as they came.

When I can find my voice,
find my breath,
I ask, "Why did they come to your call?"
"I made the cry of a wounded rabbit,"
the Bead Woman explains.
"They thought they were going
to get a tasty rabbit dinner."

The pines roar in a sudden breeze
that stirs the sky
until it reveals
the first star.
I don't want to leave this spot.

The Bead Woman says,
"I told you once that you have to learn
to call imagination to your hand.
That happens in the wild places—
outside and inside yourself.
Then you can shape it."
She pauses, then adds,
"What did you think?"

I search for words—
words even now dancing their way
toward poems—
and look up at the rising moon
that will light the way home
across these snow-graced hills.
"I think it was a mystery," I say.

But later,
when I arrive at the Farm,
still awe-stricken,
and try to tell my parents what happened,
Dad is upset, and Mom puzzled.
"What was the woman thinking?" Dad wonders.
"There was no real danger," Mom says.
"When she was younger,
Grandma Helen used to call the coyotes
all the time—all by herself.
Still," Mom adds, "Ivy certainly
should have asked us first."

It sounds strange
to hear them call the Bead Woman "Ivy,"
even though I know that is her name.
I try to tell my parents
all that I've learned

from the Bead Woman—
　　about the Greater Powers,
　　about magical places,
　　about calling and shaping imagination,
　　about mystery—
but they give me worried looks.
The feeling I walked in with—
the mystery
cradled to my heart—
vanishes.

"I don't think Eva should see this woman
anymore." Dad is pacing now. "She's filling
her head with nonsense."
"No—please!" I say. "I have to see her.
I have to!"
My parents exchange glances.
Mom says, "I think you've become too attached
to Ivy. It would be best if you get some distance—
at least for a while.
I'll call her and explain."

"Too attached!" I exclaim.
"Why is that bad?
Why is it that everything I get attached to
gets taken away?

First Grandma Helen . . .
and then Chloe.
Then Grandma Helen's watch.
Even the Farm.
And now you're taking away the Bead Woman!"

"That's enough, Eva," Dad says.
"We've made our decision."
I climb up to the Crow's Nest
and throw myself on my bed.
"I'll find a way to see her," I swear to myself.

Later that night,
when I hear Mom talking to the Bead Woman,
I sneak onto the other phone
in Grandma Helen's old room
and listen in.

"Please don't do this, Claire,"
the Bead Woman is saying.
"I've grown very fond of Eva.
I apologize about the coyotes.
It won't happen again."
Mom says, "It's more than the coyotes.
It isn't good for Eva
to have her imagination stirred up—

she's very sensitive,

as I'm sure you know.

And we don't want her getting even more

attached to you

when she's going to move away soon.

I'm so very sorry."

Mom hangs up.

For a moment there is silence on the phone.

The Bead Woman does not hang up.

"Eva?" she asks softly.

"I'm here," I whisper.

"We have to abide by your parents' wishes."

"No," I say.

"I will miss you terribly," she says.

"No," I say again.

"Always remember the Greater Powers," she adds.

"The greatest is love.

Love is something you can always call.

I will always love you."

And she hangs up.

My shoulders hunch,

and I throw the phone across the room

onto Grandma Helen's perfectly made,

perfectly empty,

bed.

Coyotes

Up in the hills
we hunt
in the moon-bright cold.

Down from the hills
we run
toward the wounded rabbit's cry.

Back to the hills
we flee
from the scent of people.

Up in the hills
we howl
at hunger denied.

A long, miserable week passes
where I hardly speak to my parents.
I lie on my bed in the Crow's Nest
and stare at my collage of the Apple Witch.
She is almost finished,
but something is missing—
I don't know what.
The Bead Woman would know.
I open my closet

and cup the hummingbird nest
with the stone egg and bird skull
in my hand.
I put the nest on the top shelf
of my bookcase,
where I can see the nest,
but not the skull.

On Saturday afternoon,
I throw a Frisbee for Sirius.
One throw sails the wrong way
toward the wild canyon
but falls just inside
the deer fence.
Will I ever be brave enough
to face the Demon Snag
or call coyotes?
I miss the Bead Woman terribly.
How I wish
I had a picture of her.

Sirius barks.
A silver Honda Civic chugs slowly up
the snow-plowed road to the house.
A stranger gets out.
Everything about him is a smile,

the curves on his cheeks,
the folds on his scarf,
the swoop of his black hair.
Sirius runs up and sniffs him,
then wags his tail—
a good sign.
Mom and Dad come out of the shed.

"My name's Ross Betta," the man says.
"I'm a reporter from the *Methow Valley News*.
I'm writing an article
about farmers here in the Methow Valley
who are facing foreclosure.
Trying to put a face on it, so to speak.
I'd like to ask you all a few questions
if you can spare the time."

Mom welcomes him as a fellow writer.
We all stomp off the snow on our boots
and troop into the house.
Soon mismatched mugs of coffee
and a plate of gingersnaps
are set on the kitchen table.
Everyone talks at once.
Mr. Betta listens and asks questions—

not only of Mom and Dad

but of me, as well.

We tell him about Achilles getting sick,

about fire blight,

the new shed,

tractor,

mortgage,

and selling Grandma Helen's watch.

I tell him about selling my poems

at the Twisp Farmer's Market.

Mr. Betta taps notes into his laptop.

After an hour, he thanks us

and asks if he can take our picture

for his story.

A strange feeling pounces in my stomach

and spreads through my fingers and toes.

I feel my hair curling like grapevines.

Something is trying to tell me something—

a voice deep inside

that is me and not me.

I listen,

touch my rose stone pendant,

and hear the heart of the Farm

in the voice of the Apple Witch.

To my surprise,

I find myself asking Mr. Betta,
"Would you like to see my Crow's Nest?"

"Oh, yes," Mom says.
"You should definitely put a picture
of Eva's Crow's Nest in your article."

I scurry up the ladder
with Mr. Betta behind me,
carrying his camera.
When he sees the Crow's Nest,
his mouth falls open.
I see my Vision Board
through his eyes
and feel a little astonished myself
at the collage of
        pictures
        paintings
        and poems
exploding across the sloping wall
from floor to ceiling.

I duck my head while
Mr. Betta reads my poem
"Bloom Time"
out loud.

Bloom Time

April Night

Stars blast cold down the night,
glittering omens of frost.
Dad searches the sky, urging clouds
to warm the blooming orchard
and save the crop.

Covered with white blossoms,
the pear trees suspend breath,
holding the promise of a year,
the hope of my family.

Past midnight
the wind machine roars in the orchard
warning of cold, of danger to the crop.
Dad wakes instantly,
as he would at the baby's cry.
He gets up—
but there's nothing more he can do.

April Morning

Sprinklers pulse shining water.
Ice hugs the pear blossom,
saving a living heart.
The orchard sparkles white shouts of joy,

spared from frost once more.
The bees begin their work,
buzzing bright songs of sun.

April Night
Stars blast cold down the night.
Dad searches the sky. . . .

"You wrote that, Eva?" Mr. Betta asks. "Honest?"
I nod, but can't meet his eyes.
"All of these poems?
And you made the collages, too?"
I nod again,
pointing out that most of the pictures
are created from old *National Geographic* magazines.
"This is so cool," Mr. Betta says,
pacing back and forth in front of the wall.
I tell him
the wall is my Vision Board,
my hope,
for saving the Farm.

He begins snapping pictures,
snapping,
snapping,
snapping.

He takes a bunch
with me standing against
the wall.
He wants to take a photo
with Achilles and me together,
but I pretend I don't hear him.

After Mr. Betta leaves,
I get an e-mail from Chloe.
I stare in surprise,
then open it.
It is an e-vite for Chloe's thirteenth birthday party
in Seattle—
an e-vite sent out to fifty people—
an e-vite without one personal word.
I'm surprised she invited me at all—
when she knows it is too far for me to go,
when she has new interests and new friends,
as Mom said.
I hit "No, I will not attend,"
and do not add a personal message.

Two weeks later
Mom rushes into the house
with a newspaper in her hands.

"Mr. Betta's article came out in today's paper,"
she cries. "Look, Eva!"
Half of the front page
is a black-and-white picture of me
standing in front of the Crow's Nest wall
all covered with my poems,
words, and pictures.
The headline says:
EVA OF THE FARM,
just the same as I sign my poems.

The paper even
printed two of my poems:
"Harvest Time" and "Always Winter."
In the article,
Mr. Betta calls me a poet and an artist.
I think of hundreds of people
reading my poems
and my heart somersaults—
almost as thrilled and terrified
as when the Bead Woman
called the coyotes.
I think of her
reading my poems too.

The next afternoon
the phone starts ringing.
Reporters from the *Wenatchee World*
and the *Seattle Times*
saw the article and want to interview me.

Me.
Evangeline DeHart.

When the phone rings again,
Mom answers,
and I see her brown eyes grow big.
When she hangs up the phone she says,
"That was KIRO-TV News in Seattle.
They want to tape an interview
with Eva to run on their program."

Me?

After talking it over alone,
Mom and Dad agree
to let me do the TV interview.

The TV crew comes
with lights and cameras.
When they see the ladder to the Crow's Nest,

they sigh.
But somehow they haul up
everything they need.
They spend a long time filming the wall.
The reporter, a woman,
is not quite so smiley as Ross Betta,
but she asks interesting questions.

On Tuesday,
when Mom and Dad are outside,
I go into Grandma Helen's room
to phone the Bead Woman.
I want to tell her to watch the TV interview,
but her answering machine picks up.
Sadness creeps over me
when I hear her recorded voice.
It sounds
far away,
and she seems
far away,
because I'm not allowed to see her.
I don't leave a message.

That night,
when the interview is scheduled to run,
we gather around our little TV and watch.

And there is the Crow's Nest
on TV!
There am I
on TV!
The entire interview lasts only a minute,
which surprises me because the reporter took
so long asking questions and filming the loft.
Mom says that is editing.
Dad says, "Let's go to Twisp
for pizza to celebrate."
So we do.
We have not gone out for dinner
in a long, long time.

At the café,
all the high chairs are full,
so we take turns holding Achilles
while we eat.
When my turn comes,
my arm feels as stiff as a branch
around him.
I haven't touched him
since he came home
from the hospital.
He's bigger than my lap remembers.
His fingers grasp my thumb—

he shakes my hand,
shakes it
and shakes it
as I have shaken the deer fence.
Mom and Dad watch us.
I stuff another piece of pepperoni pizza
into my mouth.
It tastes like something missing.

The next day
the phone rings again.
This time Dad answers.
Seattle Afternoon,
a TV talk show in Seattle,
wants me
to be a guest
on their show
in front of a live audience.

I can't believe it.

Dad says I can't go.
Mom says I can.
Dad argues that it's too much
for a twelve-year-old.
Mom argues back that it's a chance

for me to be heard,

because the show wants me

to read my poems and show pictures

of the Crow's Nest wall.

"And it would be good for me, Kurt," she adds,

"to get away for a few days."

While Mom and Dad argue,

I press my nose to the cold window,

listen to Old Man Woodstove grumble,

and look out at the orchard

all lacy with snow.

I see the deer fence,

think of the wild canyon

and the Demon Snag.

I can't do it.

I cannot

read my poems

in front of a million people.

"I can't—" I begin.

My reflection

vanishes in the fog

my breath makes on the glass.

I turn toward my parents.

"I'd be too scared. . . ."
but then the phone rings yet again.

Mom answers,
and when she hangs up,
there is an odd mixture
of relief and sadness on her face.
"That was Mrs. Jared," she says.
"Someone has just offered to buy the Farm.
She's bringing over the offer for us to review."

No!
I stare out the window again,
my heart throbbing
against
my rose stone pendant.
Again, I hear the heart of the Farm.
It is loud now,
so loud I think the whole world
must hear it.
It is the voice of the Apple Witch
telling me to be brave—
the voice of the trees
telling me to stand tall—
the voice of the river
telling me to plunge in—

the voice of the Bead Woman
telling me that sometimes we face our fears
in the most unexpected places.
They are all telling me the same thing—
do
whatever
it
takes
to save the Farm.

I leave the window
and look at my family.
"The Apple Witch wants me
to go on the TV show," I say.
Mom, Dad, and Achilles stare at me.
"The Farm itself
is telling me to go."

Sale Pending

The Gate of the Farm shuts behind me—
screaming on its hinges.

The Gate of the Farm shuts behind me—
on my way to the city.

The Gate of the Farm shuts behind me—
I will come back again, this time.

But sometime soon, too soon—
the Gate of the Farm will shut behind me forever.

As Mom and I drive
over the mountains to Seattle,
I think of the secret message I finally left
on the Bead Woman's answering machine.
"I'm going to be on TV," I told her.
"You can see me tomorrow
on *Seattle Afternoon.*
I wish—
I mean, I hope—
the Greater Powers
are helping you today."
And I hung up.

Seattle's rows of skyscrapers
are shining cliffs in the city.
Mom promises we can go up
in the Space Needle—
which I've never done before—
to meet Chloe and her mom.

Tomorrow is Chloe's thirteenth birthday.
When I think of seeing her again,
I feel like the pushmi-pullyu
from *The Story of Dr. Doolittle*.
Part of me really wants to see her,
and part of me doesn't—
because I'm scared
that Chloe doesn't want
to be my friend anymore.

The hotel where Mom and I stay
is splendiferous,
as Grandma Helen used to say.
There's a refrigerator,
called a minibar, filled with snacks,
but Mom won't let me take any,
even though *Seattle Afternoon*
is paying for the hotel.
We each have a queen-size bed
with snowy white comforters
and a zillion pillows.
A bouquet of silk roses and lilies
graces the table.
A big flat-screen TV shines
in the wall,

and Mom does let me watch
The Fellowship of the Ring.
Though I've read the book five times,
I've never seen the movie.

When Frodo stands
and declares before the council
that he will take the ring to Mordor,
though he does not know the way,
I stand and cheer.
That took not only imagination,
but courage as well.
I think that I am a little like Frodo,
reading my poems on TV
though I don't know why.
Is courage one of the Greater Powers too?
How I wish I could ask
the Bead Woman.

I'm so nervous about being on TV
that I don't sleep well,
even though the bed is a dream itself.
At eleven o'clock the next morning,
before the show,
Mom and I go to the Seattle Center.

In a glass elevator,

we zoom up

and up

and up

to the restaurant on top of the Space Needle,

and I feel as though I'm entering

another world,

a world in the clouds.

When Chloe strides in,

I hardly recognize her.

Her long curly blond hair—

her beautiful princess hair—

falls straight and smooth.

Her shirt hangs

below her jean jacket,

all sloppy.

Chloe teeters in black boots with three-inch heels—

even though she is only thirteen.

She could never walk up the canyon

in those boots,

never run through the orchard

the way we once did.

She eyes my sturdy silver boots

and rolls her eyes.

We all sit down at a table
covered with a white cloth—
Chloe and her mom on one side,
me and my mom on the other.
When I see the high prices on the menu,
my jaw falls open.
I'm glad that Chloe's mom
is treating us to celebrate Chloe's birthday.

While I eat my salmon,
Chloe asks if I have an iPhone yet.
"What is that?" I ask.
She rolls her eyes again. "Are you
on Facebook?"
I shake my head.
"Do you use Twitter?"
I am not sure what she means.
"I can do a few birdcalls," I offer.
She laughs at me,
a mean laugh, and I flush.
Mrs. Quetzal gives Chloe
a warning look and explains,
"Twitter is an Internet site
that lets you follow what your friends are doing."
I try to talk to Chloe about the Farm,

but she ignores me.
When I ask her about her life in Seattle,
she only mumbles brief answers.

During dessert
I give Chloe her birthday present
even though, in my humble opinion,
she's too mean to deserve it.
"Thanks," she says, surprised,
and opens the box.
She lifts out a sketchbook
bound in gold cloth
and opens it to the first page,
where I pasted
the picture of Chloe and me
at Camp Laughing Waters
with our hair tangled together
beneath the wildflower crowns.

"It's for your drawings," I say.
But Chloe does not answer.
She swallows hard,
drops the sketchbook back into the box,
and stabs a piece of coconut cake with her fork.
I can't take any more of her silence.
"Why won't you talk to me?" I glare at her.

"Why won't you talk about the Farm?
Or answer my e-mails?"

The coconut cake falls
from Chloe's fork
and plops onto the white tablecloth.
Her mouth opens and shuts.
"Eva deserves an answer," Mrs. Quetzal says.
Chloe wipes up the spilled cake
with her napkin
but just makes
a bigger smear on the tablecloth.
We all wait.
"Because it hurts!" Chloe exclaims at last,
glaring back at me.
"It hurts too much!
I had to forget it all,
had to leave it all behind."

I sit back, surprised.

"You'll see," Chloe adds,
a bit viciously. "You'll see
when you have to leave the Farm."
And she doesn't say another word.

When she and her mom get up to leave,
Chloe pulls on her jean jacket fast,
but her fingers stumble over the brass buttons.
She picks up the sketchbook
and presses it against her chest.
Her eyes hold mine,
and sadness spills out of them.
She takes a deep breath. "I miss . . .
roaming the canyon together.
Miss drawing.
Miss camp.
Miss . . . everything."

Then Chloe's cell phone rings,
and she answers,
and she turns her back on me,
and she walks away,
talking fast.

"Good-bye, Chloe," I whisper.

While Mom visits the restroom,
I scoot over to sit beside the window
and look out.
The Space Needle restaurant revolves

slowly around and around
so you can see the view,
ever changing,
from every direction.

I am astonished
    by the view—
    by beauty—
there is so much city—
buildings, roads, cars tiny as bugs—
but there is all of Puget Sound, too,
with its blue-green islands,
white ferryboats,
and white mountains rising beyond
the water.

I think,
as the restaurant turns and turns,
that there might be poems
hiding in this land.
When we move to the city,
I will still write.
I won't let the city change me
completely,
as it did Chloe.

And I'll work hard,
use all the Greater Powers
to make a new magical place,
in spite of great loss,
as the Bead Woman did.
I swear it.
I swear it on the Farm.

Mom comes back from the restroom.
"I'm sorry about Chloe,"
she says. "But at least now
you can move on.
Make new friends.
Come on, it's time to go."

When we get to the studio
of *Seattle Afternoon*,
everybody seems friendly.
I wear my rose stone pendant
and my silver boots—
Mom argued with me about the silver boots
but agreed when I explained
the silver boots were essential
for a heroine's courage.
I also wear a green dress
with six round, black velvet buttons

decorating the front.
We found it at the thrift store
at the Senior Center in Twisp.

Before the show starts,
Margo—
a young woman wearing skinny jeans
and black boots with three-inch heels
like Chloe's—
takes us out to see the stage.
Cushy armchairs face one another.
I look out over the empty rows of chairs
where the audience will sit,
imagine them filled with people,
and swallow hard.
I remember what the Bead Woman said
and whisper to myself,
"Conjure angels instead of monsters."

The show's host,
a man named Vic Fletcher
in a crisp gray suit
and with perfect feathery brown hair,
walks out to welcome us.
He shakes my hand.
"I've heard so much about you

and your wonderful imagination," he says.
"I'm looking forward
to hearing your poems."
His eyes are kind.
I wonder if his hair would move in a breeze.

We go backstage
to wait for the show to start.
I ask if Mom is going out onstage with me,
and Margo says yes.
Still, this is almost as scary
as going up the canyon alone.
Almost.

Fifteen minutes later I hear applause.
Then all of a sudden
I'm walking out
onto the stage
into the lights
with the big cameras
pointed straight
at me.
The audience is a field of faces—
eyes, so many eyes—
stare
at me.

I stop.

"Come on," Mom whispers.
I clutch my rose stone pendant for courage
and walk up to Vic Fletcher.
We all sit down
in the cushy armchairs.

Vic Fletcher asks a hundred questions
about the Farm,
my poems,
and the Crow's Nest wall.
He is easy to talk to.
Soon I'm chattering away
while Mom smiles.

But when Vic Fletcher asks me to read
two of my poems out loud,
my throat closes.
I sit silently for a moment,
my hands shaking so hard
the paper I hold rattles.
All the eyes stare up at me,
and I feel naked.
Then the audience starts to clap,
encouraging me.

For the Farm, I think,
be brave to save the Farm.
I take a deep breath
and stand tall,
as I did when the coyotes
came running toward me.
I read "The Fortune-Teller" first.

The Fortune-Teller

In the snowy patch of spring,
the squirrel with half a tail—

   close getaway from a hawk?

   breathless escape from a coyote?
nibbles the husk from an old walnut,
turning it like a crystal ball
in his paws to read the future.

The other squirrels scold him
for his daydreaming,
urge him to get busy
digging up buried nuts.

But the half-tailed fortune-teller
sees summer unfold
in the walnut's heart

and chitters a prophecy—
of warmth,
of green husked nuts falling
like rain from the trees.

The other squirrels gather round,
listen and hope and discover
that a story can be filling too,
that even a dreamy, half-tailed squirrel
has a place among them.

The audience claps when I finish.
Then I read "Sun Daisies."

Sun Daisies
After the snow,
before the heat,
sun daisies blister tales of gold
amid the sagebrush and bitterbrush
on the wind-shorn hills.

Cows gorge
upon the petaled glory—
turning their milk so gold
that Rumpelstiltskin

scampers up
to do mischief.

Imprisoned with an impossible task
I toil at the spinning wheel.
Can I spin poems into gold
to save the Farm?

Rumpelstiltskin will not help—
he already has the firstborn sons and daughters
of ten thousand princesses to feed.

My fingers bleed upon the spindle.
No princess, I
do not fall asleep and dream of princes.
No one will rescue me.

Without magic,
without aid,
I spin and spin.
Wishing I had so strong a stuff as straw
to change,
I spin instead
my hopes and dreams
into a thread of words—

my last best chance
for happily ever after.

The audience claps again—
some people cheer.
I sit down,
wobbly as Jell-O,
glad that's over,
glad I found the courage
to do it.
I take a deep breath.

"We have a picture of Eva's Crow's Nest wall
on the screen behind me," Vic Fletcher says.
I turn
and see my loft wall projected
huge,
in vibrant color.
I gasp,
because I see—
    not the pictures
    not the calligraphy
    not the words
    not the colors—
but the black patches.

They look like the patches
covering the woodpecker damage
on our house.
They look like the black velvet buttons
on my green dress.

Vic Fletcher asks more questions,
and I mumble answers.
When he asks, "What do those black patches
represent, Eva?"
I can't speak,
because in my mind looms the image
of the Demon Snag pointing his black ball
at me.
I can't speak,
because suddenly I know
the Demon Snag
is in me.

In me.

Mom sees my distress and says,
"Oh, the black patches are where Eva
covered up her baby brother's pictures
when she got mad at him."

A ball of fire singes my stomach,
and I stare at Mom, horrified.
Horrified that she knew.
Horrified that she said it on TV
for a million people to hear,
for the Bead Woman to hear.

Why did she say that?
How could she do that to me?
My own mom.
I stare at her,
but she looks away,
and for the first time in my life
I feel all alone in the world.

Vic Fletcher leans forward.
"Why were you mad at your baby brother, Eva?"
I take a deep breath
and wonder if a demon voice
will boom from my mouth,
but only a whisper comes out.
"Because he got sick."
Even though it's my own voice,
I can't say another word.
Mom explains how we had extra bills

from Achilles's pneumonia,
and so had to put the Farm up for sale.

"So you blame your brother
for losing your beloved farm?" Vic Fletcher asks softly.
"No!" I cry. "It's the Demon Snag's fault!"
"Who is the Demon Snag?" Vic Fletcher asks.

I want to run away,
run far, far away
from all the eyes—
but I cannot run
from the Demon Snag in me.
So I slouch in the chair
and pull at one of the black buttons
on my dress.

After a silence,
Vic Fletcher says,
"The DeHart family is going to lose the farm
that Eva loves so much,
not only because of her brother's illness,
but also because of the poor economy.
Like so many families in America today,
they are facing foreclosure.
I want to thank you, Eva, and Mrs. DeHart,

for sharing your story
on *Seattle Afternoon* today."

And the show is over.
After I stammer my thanks
to Vic Fletcher and Margo,
Mom and I get back in the car
and start the long drive back
over the Cascade Mountains
to the Methow Valley.

In the car,
I ignore Mom
and try to read my favorite book,
Hattie Big Sky,
about another heroine—
like Meg, Joan of Arc, and Evangeline—
a heroine who loved her land, like me,
and lost it,
but gained something greater.

All I can think of, though,
is how a million people saw my shame,
how the Bead Woman will no longer love me,
how Mom embarrassed me,
how the Demon Snag is in me,

how I will never be a heroine now,
how everything is lost.
My fingers twist and pull
one of the black velvet buttons on my dress
until it comes off.
I fling it on the car floor
and start pulling on another one.

When we get home,
I rush up the ladder
to the Crow's Nest,
unzip the green dress,
and throw it on the floor.
Not one black velvet button is left.

With my back to my Vision Board wall,
I pull on a T-shirt, sweater, and jeans.
I slap the blue hat Grandma Helen made on my head,
jam my silver boots back on my feet,
and polish my rose stone necklace
with my breath.
A minute later
I march to the canyon gate
in the deer fence.
I unlatch the gate
and throw it wide open.

Sirius wags his tail beside me,
hoping for a walk up the canyon.
"No, Sirius," I say, rubbing his ears.
"You are a good and noble dog,
but I have to go
by myself."
I stride through the gate
and close it behind me.
I start up the canyon
alone—
but I take all of the Farm
with me.
"Apple Witch, help me,"
I whisper.
"Bead Woman, help me."

I carry a stick to fight
cougars and bears and coyotes
and the silence of the winter wood.
Not one branch waves—
the wind is dead.
Creature tracks scar
the snow.
Up and up I go,
looking everywhere—
ahead of me,

behind me,

left,

right,

everywhere.

At last, in the first meadow,

where the bones of the dead deer

lie in the snow,

I stop, brace myself, and look south.

On top of the hill,

the Demon Snag rears.

"I'm not like you!" I shout.

The Demon Snag seems to grow taller.

His arm holding the black ball

points straight at me.

"No!" I cry. "I love Achilles!

And love is the greatest power

of them all!"

Snapping branches

shatter the silence.

I freeze.

A bear lumbers out

through the aspens—
a brown monster smeared
against the white trunks.
My heart pounds.
My breath stops.
I ache to run,
but know that is the worst thing
to do.
So I raise my stick.

The bear sniffs,
stops,
looks right at me.
It is the bear who raids
our plum tree!
I know because his right ear
is missing.
As he takes a step toward me,
the sun hums its roundness,
breaking though the clouds.
Light pulses, sings,
firing the bear's muzzle silver,
bedazzling the canyon.
I seem to hear the Apple Witch
laughing with joy.

The voice of the Farm rises inside me,
roaring my heart alive.

"I put you in a poem," I whisper
to the bear.
"Why aren't you asleep in your den?
It's too early for plums."
Sniffing again,
the bear swings his head.
Then he turns
and runs away
up the canyon.

As I watch him go,
I name him
the wild, magical spirit
of the canyon—
an angel
instead of a monster.
And then I understand
that the spirit of the Farm
in me is magical too—
understand
that imagination
is my power
and my strength.

I hold up my rose stone pendant,

summon the Greater Powers,

point my stick at the Demon Snag,

and call out a spell of my own—

    "I am Eva of the Farm!

    Hear me!

    In the name of all the Greater Powers,

    I banish you, Demon Snag,

    from my heart!

    Banish you

    from this canyon.

    I name you Good Wizard.

    Save us all!"

Echoes boomerang

through all the hidden caverns,

down every hole and den,

into hide and rattle and maw.

The wind rises now,

and the whole canyon springs alive

with waving branches.

I throw away my stick,

because if that bear had charged,

what good would a stick have done?

The stick is a chimera.

Is banishing the Demon Snag from my heart
a chimera too?

I hear a cry.
An eagle skims the sky—
circling, circling,
crying hope.

I watch it,
then pick up the stick.
and twirl it, because,
after all,
chimeras do have power—
the Greater Power of Hope.

Back home,
I climb up to the Crow's Nest
and attack my Vision Board.
I tear off a black patch,
then another and another
until every single one is gone.
Stubborn black shreds stick to the wall,
so I scrape my fingernails raw
to get every bit.
I will replace the ruined pictures
of Achilles.

I cram all the black paper into a bag,
carry it down the ladder,
and stuff it
inside Old Man Woodstove.
Achilles stands in his playpen.
I scoop him up
while Old Man Woodstove
cackles.

"Achilles," I whisper.
"I love you. I'm so sorry.
Will you forgive me?"
As I smell his scent
of applesauce and Johnson's shampoo,
I know that what I almost lost
was far more precious than the Farm.
Achilles grins his lopsided grin
and laughs. "Va, play!"

We do.

During the next two weeks,
I wander through the orchard
every day after school—
savoring the last hours
left at the Farm

before the sale closes.

I gather in the magic,

storing it inside me,

so I can make wherever we go next

magic too.

How much magic is in the place,

I wonder,

and how much is in what you bring

to the place?

I guess I'll find out.

Mom spends hours in the shed.

One night I wake up at three a.m.

and see a light still shining in the office.

A coyote howls,

then yips on the far side

of the deer fence.

I wonder if the Bead Woman is awake too.

I needed everything she taught me

to fight

the Demon Snag.

Will I ever see her again?

I get up,

go to my bookcase,

and find the hummingbird's nest

on the top shelf.

With one finger,
I trace the delicate bird skull
and then the polished stone egg.
Life and death together.
I fall asleep with the nest beside me
on the bedside table,
no longer afraid
of my imagination.

On Saturday,
Dad brings a stack of letters
from the post office.
"They're all addressed to you," he says, smiling.
I count them: fifty-nine letters,
some addressed to Eva DeHart,
some to "The Little Girl Who Writes Poetry."
People sent them to *Seattle Afternoon*,
which forwarded them on to me.

I sit on the floor
in front of Old Man Woodstove
and pick out a letter to open.
The lavender envelope I choose
has ruffled edges on the flap
and smells of lilies.
It is from Mrs. Ruby L. Evans

of Moses Lake, Washington.
I unfold a piece of lavender paper
and read the letter out loud.

Dear Eva,

I saw you today on *Seattle Afternoon*. And I must say,
your story touched my heart. What a fine example
of America's young people you are. I live on a farm
too, here in Moses Lake, where we grow wheat.
I loved your poems—especially the one about the
fortune-teller—what a wonderful imagination you
have! I have enclosed a stamp and would dearly love
it if you would send me a copy of that poem. I hope
you and your family get to keep your farm. Thank
you so much for brightening my day.

Best Wishes,
Ruby L. Evans

I read the letter to Mom and Dad and Achilles.

"I don't understand," I blurt.
"Everyone saw
how horrible I am. Blaming Achilles

for losing the Farm.
Why would they write to me?"
"You're just human, Eva," Dad says.
"That's all people saw,
and it touched their hearts."

Mom says, "I'm sorry for revealing something
so personal, Eva. I shouldn't have done that."
I ask, not looking at her,
"Why did you do it, Mom?"
She sighs. "Because I was mad at you
for being so angry with Achilles.
I swallow hard. "Are you still mad?"
"Oh no, Eva. Can you forgive me?"
But I can't, not yet.
There's something I have to know first.
And I ask the question
I have been unable to ask for months.
"Do you really want to leave the Farm, Mom?"
She smiles. "Run up to the Crow's Nest for a minute."
I look at her,
but she only says, "Go on."

I climb up the ladder
to the Crow's Nest,
and then I see it:

the spinning wheel—
all repaired—
sitting proudly in one corner,
the oak golden in the winter sun
rampaging through the skylight.
No blue sheet covers it now.

I throw my arms around the spinning wheel
and cry.
The rim feels as smooth as the skin
on the inside of Achilles's wrist.
On the floor sits a bag of wool.
I spin the wheel,
watching the spokes make a blur
of hope.
I can almost see the golden thread
of my imagination
streaming out.
I can almost see Grandma Helen.

At least I will have some piece of her
when we move to Seattle.
I will take the spinning wheel
even if I have to leave everything else
behind.

I climb back down the ladder.
Mom is still smiling.
Dad stands with his arms around her.
I ask Mom, "What made you finally decide to fix it?"
She is silent, then says,
"You did.
Through your eyes,
through your poems and pictures,
I've fallen in love
with the Farm all over again."

Something in me melts then,
and I do forgive her.

Mom adds, "I've sold
a series of seven articles, too."
"So that's what you've been doing
out in the shed!" I exclaim.
"Writing and fixing the spinning wheel.
We'll learn to spin, Achilles!"
I whirl him around and around.
"We'll spin and spin and spin!"
"'Pin and 'pin!" he exclaims.

"Eva," Dad says. "I have a present for you too."

I take a box from him and open it.

Inside is a stack

of Canson calligraphy paper.

I look up, surprised,

and see Dad grinning.

"I was wrong," he says.

"Poetry may not save the polar bears,

but it has helped this family.

You've proven that—in my humble opinion."

And he looks at Mom.

I throw my arms around him.

"We have more news," Mom says.

"We just found out this morning

that the people who wanted to buy the farm

could not get their loan approved."

My heart leaps. "So?" I ask.

"So the deal fell through," Dad says.

"The Farm is not sold."

I can hardly bear to ask, "Are we staying, then?"

"We don't know yet," Mom says.

"The money from the articles will help,

and we may get a grant from a foundation

that helps with children's medical bills.

But we just don't know yet.

You'll have to live
with the uncertainty."
I say, "You mean live with hope.
It's one of the Greater Powers."
Mom smiles. "Yes, with hope."

"Open another letter," says Dad.
I pick up an envelope with
a crayon apple tree scribbled on it,
from Clyde Stevens of Portland, Oregon.

Dear Little Girl Who Writes Poems,
I write poems, too. I am nine. Please write back.

Clyde Stevens
Poet

My whole family—
even Sirius—
sits around me on the floor
as I read letter after letter out loud.
Some have poems and drawings from kids.
Everyone says they hope
we can keep the Farm.

Surely all that hope is a powerful force.

Then one letter springs out,
from Ivy Marie Bauer
on pale gray speckled paper
like stone.
"It's from the Bead Woman," I say,
and look at my parents.
"May I open it?"
They nod.

Dear Eva,
Your parents gave me permission to write to you.
You were brilliant on *Seattle Afternoon*, brilliant and
breathtaking—your poems, your self, your heart.
What courage you have. How much I learned from
watching you. How proud I am of you.

I can't recall if I ever told you that thulite—the stone
I made your pendant out of—has a special gift. It
helps with new beginnings in love.

Wishing you joy, hope, imagination, and love,
The Bead Woman

I look at my parents.

"Please," I say. "I have to see her again. Please."

"I had a long talk with Ivy," Mom says,
"when she called to ask permission
to send you the letter. I understand
everything better now.
And I think it will be all right, Eva."

I am light,
light as a winged seed
dancing on the wind.
I open my arms.
"There is something I have to do," I say.
My family watches me put on my coat
and silver boots.
"Where are you going?" asks Mom.
"Up the canyon," I say.
Mom and Dad stare in surprise.
"Alone?" Dad asks.
"No. I'm taking Achilles in the baby backpack."
My parents look at each other,
then nod, pleased.

A few minutes later,
I walk toward the gate in the deer fence

and see the little tree Dad planted there
during the storm last fall.
The tree is small to be a sentinel at the edge
of the wild world.
And I think that all the little trees he plants
are Dad's hope.

We all need hope.

I open the gate in the deer fence
and tramp up the wild canyon
as snow lazes down,
licking the branches with white icing.
Achilles chatters on my back
in his white snowsuit and hat,
and though I bend forward from his weight,
he seems as light as a snowflake.

We pass the grove of ponderosa pines,
their needles speckled white.
We pass the grove of aspens,
their bare branches white as fish bones
against the blue sky.
Achilles's breath makes puffs
of white over my left shoulder.

Has the whole world turned white?

"Look, Achilles," I say.
"Look at everything!"
We reach the meadow where the deer
and her baby died,
the scattered bones lumps of white.

I kneel carefully
and paw through the snow
until I find a backbone.
It is clean and beautiful.
I will take it home
and glue it in the hand
of the Apple Witch,
and she will finally
be complete.

"Look even at this, Achilles,"
I say, holding up the bone.
"At the wheel of life turning,
and don't be afraid.
Don't let anything stop you."

And I know,
that all that I thought was lost

is simply a spoke in the turning wheel,

ever changing.

Grandma Helen was a spoke,

and Chloe

and the watch

and the Bead Woman

and even the Farm.

They are the spokes,

and I am the wheel

that keeps spinning,

always spinning—

holding them all.

I look up

and see the white snout

of Heaven's Gate Mountain

nosing through the clouds.

Slowly I turn toward the south hill.

I blink

and press my rose stone pendant

against my heart.

The Demon Snag has changed.

It—*he*

sparkles white

in a snow robe stitched

with diamonds.
A white ball glitters in his hand,
pointing at me.
"Good Wizard!" I shout.
"The Demon Snag is banished.
The Farm is saved forever
for Achilles and me."

I know it is true.
Even if there is not enough money,
even if we have to leave the Farm,
it will never be lost,
because I have captured it
in my poems and my heart.
It will live forever
by the Greater Power
of my imagination.

I will always be Eva of the Farm.

The Greater Powers

Achilles and me—
hunted wild asparagus in the moonlight,
down by the trunks of the pear trees,
laughing round and round the blossoming orchard,
snagging our hair in the beckoning branches.

Achilles and me—
crept through the grass, then sprang,
seizing the firm ones, not withered by frost,
choosing the tight ones,
not gone to seed, to seed, to seed.

Achilles and me—
danced and gathered and ate them,
stalked them and snapped them,
filled up our baskets,
not one escaped us.

Achilles and me—
hunted wild asparagus
and sang with the coyotes until the violet dawn,
until the violet dawn roared down,
until the violet dawn.